UNTOUCHED

LAUREN HAWKEYE

Book design by Maureen Cutajar
www.gopublished.com

eISBN: 978-1-625175-22-9
ISBN: 978-1-942356-12-7

This one's for Jia Gayles, for putting up with me.

UNTOUCHED

CHAPTER ONE

IT WAS A RARE cold day in Arizona when Alexa Kendrick made her decision.

The air that she heaved in and out of her lungs was thin and dry, seemingly doing little to replenish her breath as she scrambled up the last bit of rocky path and onto the isolated ledge.

Thigh muscles burning, she lowered herself to the ground. Studded with sharp stones and stubbled with dry grass that poked through the thin spandex of her yoga pants, it was hardly the most comfortable place to while away the hours, and yet Alexa had done just that, over and over again in the past months.

The world stretched out below her, a breathtaking panorama of the purest blue set against the rust and umber tones of the rocky earth. For the first time in nearly a year, her fingers twitched at her side, scraping through the dust as they instinctively reached for a paintbrush.

If she had one here, she'd start a landscape. Something that tried to capture the overwhelming sense of being just another cog in the clock of the world, of being an infinitesimal part of something so very much bigger than herself.

She would paint it in oil—it had to be oil, to capture the undiluted hues that surrounded her. A pencil wouldn't do.

The thought made her laugh out loud, startling a small lizard who had scuttled over to investigate the giant human who had invaded his territory.

Here she was, plotting out her next painting, when she'd done nothing for a year except serve beer and mediocre chicken entrees to strangers at a chain restaurant—to her mother's abject horror, of course.

A full year since the car accident. How had that much time slipped by, rushing past in a pastel haze that never sharpened into anything more substantial?

The accident itself remained blank, void of words, of color, of anything really. She'd healed physically, but how did one move past something so life changing that yet seemed to not exist, at least in her memory?

But it did exist—she had the angry red scars on her pale skin to prove it... and the guilt. Oh yes, if her memory was an intangible shade of nothing, the guilt—the guilt was the most vivid of crimsons, a deep blood red that was impossible to ignore.

She was that blood, and flesh, and bone, and she was here. Others were not, and however much it weighed on her mind—why her? Why not them?

Well. The fact remained that she was here, and that time marched on. She couldn't exactly spend the rest of her life ensconced in her mother's house, in a job that she performed solely because it provided busywork for her hands.

Her body was healed. She was going to have to accept that her mind might always have this great gaping hole in it—a hole that was the best thing for her, her mother continually assured her.

The fingers twitching for a paintbrush were just the latest evidence of her itchiness. It was time to get back to the business of being Alexa Kendrick.

If only she knew who that was anymore.

Brushing dry crumbs of dust off of her fingers, Alexa unzipped the pocket of her windbreaker and pulled out her cell phone. Her mother had objected to these solitary hikes of hers until Alexa had assured her that she never went far enough to escape cell range. The ledge on which she perched offered a view of a small canyon that hid the entire city of Phoenix from view, but it was never far away, too vast to be swallowed forever.

Pulling up her contact list, Alexa selected the listing for her agent. "Hey, Jia," she smiled reflexively when the other woman answered.

"*Tell* me you have something for me." Jia's throaty rasp worked its way through the line.

"Hello to you, too." Alexa winced at her agent's words as a thin trickle of annoyance made its presence known.

"That was tacky, wasn't it?" Jia sounded contrite, and Alexa could just picture her grimacing into her phone, the expression pulling her smooth mocha skin tight. Never able to sit still, she would be pacing, quite literally wearing a path in the carpet of her office as she took her calls and answered emails from her smart phone.

Jia was the woman who had discovered Alexa's art, and their relationship was at the five year mark. Still, Alexa could never quite forget that theirs was a relationship built on money.

"Well, I can't blame you for asking." Nibbling on her thumbnail, Alexa smiled wryly to herself.

The major gallery in Phoenix that carried her work had sold the last piece six months ago, and the other galleries across the country, the ones that had carried a select few of her works, had also been depleted. Alexa had nothing to replace them with... at least, not yet.

"Well, you know I'll be here when you're ready," Jia rumbled, her voice sounding like nothing so much as a big cat's purr. Yet, Alexa couldn't miss the note that said the other woman hoped that Alexa would be ready *soon.*

"I'm actually thinking that a change of scenery might help." Alexa worried her thumbnail with her teeth, realized she was doing it, and scowled down at her hands. Because of her job as a painter, they once had been a disaster, always stained with a million Technicolor smudges. But now they were smooth, perfect, and seemed to belong to someone else entirely.

"A change of scenery? A trip?" Jia squawked in Alexa's ear, and her eardrums rang. "Go. Go, go, go! Chase that creative spark. Where are you going?"

"Have you heard of Florence?" Her words sounded far lighter than they felt. Jia was the first person she was telling of her plans... in fact, she hadn't entirely made up her mind until she'd pulled out her cell.

This was it. No turning back.

"Florence?" The surprise in the other woman's voice was clear. There was a weighted pause, during which Alexa counted four deep breaths. "You mean... isn't that the place with all the prisons?"

"Indeed." Alexa tried to keep her tone light, but inside she felt anything but. The choice of destination was strange, certainly, but it wasn't at all random.

"Not to be critical," Jia continued, a frown clear in her words, "but what about someplace more... colorful? Bermuda? Mexico? Tonga?"

"Those all sound great," Alexa replied, and she was mostly telling the truth. They would have sounded great up until she'd learned of her reason to go to Florence. Now, she would have felt like she was wasting time if she jetted off to lounge on a beach. "But this isn't a vacation, per se. It turns out I... might have family there."

Swallowing thickly, she spat out the last two words, the ones that she still couldn't quite believe. "A sister, in fact."

"A *sister*?" Predictably, Jia wanted details. She knew that Alexa was an only child, had been raised by her single mother. "What? How?"

"It may not be legit." The warning was more for herself than for anyone else. It was also a way to close the conversation. "I just wanted you to know where I was going. I'll let you know if the change of scenery gets the paint flowing again."

As she ended the call, Alexa felt a surge of excitement. It was good, having told someone—it was real.

Standing, she brushed the dampness of her palms off on the thighs of her pants, noted the thin sheen of sweat on her forehead despite the chill. She'd been more worked up about the decision than she'd thought, but now that it had been made, a strange sort of peace settled in.

Placing her hands above her head, Alexa stretched out her arms, her torso as she took one final look down into the canyon.

Rather than finding the solace that the mountains had brought her over the last year, for the first time she felt as though the yawning landscape was closing in.

She'd lived in Phoenix for her entire life, and until the accident, had never questioned any part of her existence. Maybe the need for more would have come anyway, or maybe the crash had changed her more than she thought, but either way, as she watched the cold wind send spirals of biscuit colored dust dancing in the thin air, she knew.

It was time to go.

*   *   *

THE INTERIOR OF HER mother's house was set to a perfectly comfortable temperature, just like it always was. Alexa couldn't remember a time that she'd been uncomfortable within these walls, no matter the searing heat or, like now, frigid air outside.

Even though she'd moved back in a year ago, right after her release from the hospital, she still thought of it as her mother's house. In fact, she'd always thought of it that way, though she'd in no way had a bad childhood.

But as she moved through the halls, noted the collections of crystal vases, of china plates that had remained the same over the years, she could see no mark of herself anywhere. While that had always seemed normal to her, in the last few weeks it had become more than a little stifling.

Tracy Cunningham was in her greenhouse, as she always was at this time of day. The glassed-in extension of the large house was deliciously warm and moist, reminiscent of one of those tropical locales that Jia had been urging Alexa to go to. That thick air was filled with the sweet scent of her mother's prize orchids, which were arranged in stunning symmetrical displays along each wall.

Standing at the spotless stainless steel sink, soaking the roots of a cymbidium, was Tracy herself, dressed for gardening in dark jeans, a fitted white blouse, and pale pink gloves. Her hair, a cool blonde that contrasted sharply with Alexa's deep chestnut brown, was back in a sleek chignon that made her daughter feel, as always, just the slightest bit messier, dirtier, larger, louder. As did the inevitable surge of love twined with frustration.

She loved her mother, of course she did. This was, after all, the woman who had, after the horridly un-athletic Alexa had humiliated herself at a track meet, went out and purchased a slip and slide for their backyard, proclaiming that the strip of yellow plastic was Alexa's ribbon, and the best one there was. This was the woman who had once grabbed the ear of a teenage boy and threatened to knee him in the nuts when she'd found him throwing rocks at Alexa as she cowered behind a bush.

She was also the woman who frowned disapprovingly over the consumption of dessert, and who became furious at the slightest sign of disrespect, and who infuriatingly ignored opinions that weren't her own.

Alexa knew she was about to throw herself headfirst into the latter. Still, she pressed on, closing the glass door behind her rather than risking a treatise on the ideal environment for orchids.

"I thought you worked today." The slight sniff and sarcastic emphasis of the word worked were not lost on Alexa, who felt her spine stiffening, despite the multiple lectures she'd given herself on the subject.

Her mom was actually being quite good, considering. Having an artist for a daughter had been puzzling enough, though Tracy seemed to have comes to terms with it once Alexa had started seeing some success from her painting. But waitressing at a chain restaurant just to keep herself busy—and out of the house—had turned into a not so silent war between them. Only by threatening to move out had Alexa won, but she saw now that she shouldn't have used that as a threat.

She was as healed as she was ever likely to be, and it was time to go.

"I'm taking some time off from the restaurant," Alexa said slowly as she skirted the shelves of blooms.

Her mother, both hands holding the now sodden weight of the orchid, turned her head and flashed a smile full of relief.

"Oh, Alexa, I can't tell you how happy that makes me." Tracy nodded with apparent satisfaction. "I know we've had our differing opinions over that job, but I'm so glad that you're coming around."

"I'm not quitting." Alexa had learned early on that the best way to have a *differing opinion* with her mother was to do it head on. "But I do have something to tell you."

"You're not pregnant, are you?" Droplets of soil heavy water flew as Tracy whirled, aghast.

"Oh, for the..." Alexa couldn't keep herself from rolling her eyes, though she knew it would irritate the hell out of her mother. "No. No, I am not pregnant. Though it's great to know how thrilled you'd be if I was."

"Don't be sarcastic, Alexa. It doesn't suit you." Tracy pursed her lips before turning back to her work. "Now. What did you have to tell me?"

A snaking tendril of apprehension whipped through Alexa, surprising her with its intensity. It was almost ... foreboding.

But she'd made her choice, so she shook it off and spat it out.

"I'm going on a trip," she said finally, drawing out the last word ever so slightly, "to Florence."

Alexa watched her mother closely as she announced her destination, and though she almost missed it, it was there... the slightest stiffening of the spine. The reaction was almost indiscernible, but it was enough to answer Alexa's unspoken question.

"There's nothing there for you, Alexa." As if that reaction hadn't happened at all, Tracy turned back to her orchids. Alexa watched for a long moment, noting the care with which her mother treated the delicate plants.

Finally, she spoke. "My father was from Florence."

"Your father is dead." Tracy cast Alexa a sharp look before visibly forcing herself to relax.

"I know that." Alexa stepped back, affronted. "I just..."

She shouldn't have to explain it. She was an adult, and she could go where she pleased, technically. That had never been the way that things ran in this house. She told her mother everything.

Until now, withholding details felt just the same as lying. To counteract the guilt, she decided to ask questions before she could be asked them herself.

"Did we live right in town?" The truth was, she'd always been curious about the small town where her father had grown up. Who wouldn't be intrigued—and kind of freaked out—by a place that boasted nine county, state and federal prisons, and two private ones? It was kind of creepy. "How did you two meet?"

Tracy had always been closed mouthed about the father that had died when Alexa was a small child, and now was no exception. She pursed her lips and shook her head in response to the questions.

"I know you're feeling trapped," Tracy didn't turn to look at her daughter as she spoke, instead continuing her work with her orchids, "and I also understand why you're curious about your roots. But Florence is a dreary little tow that runs on the prison's clock. Go and you'll be back within a day."

Alexa opened her mouth to respond, determined—even if nothing came of this supposed family connection, she was planning some time away. It wasn't all prisons, after all—Florence was a well preserved, historic little town.

But Tracy wasn't done. "And I'm just not sure how I feel about you driving that far yet. I'll worry." Here she did look at Alexa, and though Alexa knew that it was deliberate, the resultant wave of guilt was bright and real.

"I'll be fine." Alexa made sure that her voice was firm. Sensing the imminent argument, she decided that retreat was her best option. She headed up to the room from her childhood, sinking down on the edge of her bed, half braced for her mother to follow her and continue their discussion—locks were not a part of this household.

But Tracy didn't appear, leaving Alexa alone with her

thoughts. As she sat there, looking around the spacious, beautiful room, noting how alien her belongings looked amongst the elegant decor, she knew deep down that something big was about to change.

The answer to so many of her questions lay in Florence. She was sure of it. Though she may not stay there for very long, she wasn't sure that she was ever coming back here.

*   *   *

TRACY'S HANDS SHOOK AS she made her way to her room, pausing for a moment when she passed Alexa's shut door.

Part of her wanted to do everything it took to keep her here, even if that meant tying her down to her bed until she came to her senses.

But she'd learned long ago that people had a will of their own, and there was only so much you could take upon yourself without going crazy.

She was greeted by the faint smell of her own perfume as she pushed through the heavy door. The room was cool and dim, lit only by one skinny ribbon of light that poured through the crack between the heavy curtains.

She stood in the dark, the air seeming to press down on her body. Belatedly, she realized that the pruning shears that normally sat by the sink in her greenhouse were still in her hands.

Her entire body jerked as her hands tightened on the metallic handles. The emotions swelling beneath her skin needed an outlet, and she was seized with the urge to lift those shears, to hack away at her own hair.

A momentary inner war resulted in her setting the blades decisively down on her dresser. She was not a woman given to foolish urges. In fact, she'd given in to one exactly once. That capitulation had resulted in a beautiful daughter, so she could never regret it.

But now that daughter had unknowingly put her in a very bad place.

Tracy had to make some decisions. There were things she'd decided that Alexa never needed to know, but if her daughter was going to Florence, then it was unlikely that that was a coincidence. Something had sparked her interest—something like a memory, perhaps—and that was dangerous.

True, Alexa might go and come back none the wiser. But the other potential result?

She could go and learn things that would shatter the egg-shell wall that Tracy had so carefully reinforced.

Should she warn her?

But Alexa still wasn't fully recovered, no matter her daughter's thoughts on the matter. Though she was so much better than when Tracy had first seen her, white and broken in that narrow hospital bed, she was under no illusions that her daughter was fully healed.

Tracy wasn't at all certain that Alexa could handle the full truth, at least not yet.

So she decided to remain silent.

For now.

CHAPTER TWO

IT WAS ONLY A SIXTY mile drive from Phoenix to Florence. Alexa had expected to feel some kind of dread, or at least mild trepidation, when she'd turned the sturdy SUV onto the freeway. The vehicle itself was a reminder of her accident, if one could have reminders of things that they didn't remember.

She'd once driven a small, sporty little car. But Tracy had purchased the larger vehicle when Alexa had first announced her intentions to try driving again—she'd insisted that her daughter would feel safer in it.

Though she resented her mother's overprotectiveness, secretly Alexa had agreed with her. She'd thought that a more solid vehicle surrounding her would feel good.

But she'd never felt any hesitation over getting behind the wheel again. Not even a whisper of the expected fear.

Those feelings held as she pulled out of the city and onto the freeway—further than she'd driven herself in a year. Nope, instead of fear, she'd felt freedom—an invisible yoke lifting off of her shoulders, setting her free.

The miles passed quickly, but instead of being a blur, the scenery was in glorious high definition—sepia and carmine, turquoise and olive. The colors settled in Alexa's mind's eye like paint on a canvas, the almost forgotten sensation of inspiration a surprise as light and effervescent as champagne bubbles.

Instead of weighing heavily on her mind, the knowledge that her case of paints and brushes was in the trunk felt good, felt right. Gave her some control. Despite what was taking her to Florence—and despite her mother's assurances that she'd find nothing worthwhile there—Alexa was sure that if nothing else, she'd break through the mental block that had held her talent captive since the accident.

Not being able to paint had been like losing a limb. When she was finally able to express herself again in the way that suited her best—then, she would feel complete. Though the pictures in her mind's eyes were decidedly more... grey... than they had been before her accident.

Alexa refused to allow that to depress her, to ruin the sparkly feeling that freedom and creativity had started inside of her. There was no pressure on her talent here.

She didn't have to paint. In fact, she didn't have to do anything.

Except, perhaps, get to know the sister that she'd never known existed.

*   *   *

Two days earlier...

POLYESTER WAS NOT A material suited to physical exertion or heat. Which made Alexa wonder why the uniforms at the Boxtree were made of the stuff.

She was wiping perspiration from her forehead with a clean bar towel when Lyndsey rounded the corner by the ice dispenser. Her pretty blonde friend looked as warm as she felt, her normally immaculate makeup wilting a bit in the heat.

"There's someone at table seven asking for you." Grabbing an empty glass, Lyndsey scooped a cup full of ice, then pressed it to her cheeks. "God. It might be worth losing the tips, just to work someplace with AC."

Alexa felt the familiar pang of guilt as she nodded in agreement. Lyndsey was a single mom who needed every dollar she could get, and ugly, hot uniforms or not, the fact that Boxtree was a chain meant they were busy, which in turn meant steady tips.

Alexa? She was here because she'd needed something to do to keep her hands busy, and because she knew that her mother would never set foot in a place that sold nachos and cheese fries. This gave her some much needed freedom.

But she certainly didn't need the money. But though Lyndsey was the closest thing she had to a friend, she wasn't about to tell her that. She hadn't even told her about the car accident that had landed her in the hospital.

What could she tell, after all? She didn't remember it.

"Is it a regular?" Alexa asked absently as she followed Lyndsey's example and scooped up some ice. The chill of the glass was heavenly against her fevered skin.

"It's a woman. Our age, red hair." Sighing heavily, Lyndsey tossed the remainder of her ice in the large metal sink and placed her glass in the dirty dish bin, then picked up her tray again. "Never seen her in here before."

"All right." Faintly puzzled, Alexa reluctantly emptied out her own cup of ice. Tucking her notepad into the pocket of her half apron, she left the ice dispenser area and crossed the room to table seven.

She wasn't sure what, exactly, she'd been expecting after Lyndsey's comments. Maybe someone she'd known in high school. Or... something.

She was slightly unnerved to find a woman maybe a few years older than herself, waiting with a slightly hostile expression on her face. The woman had red hair and creamy pale skin, but when she looked up as Alexa approached, it was her eyes that got to Alexa.

They were familiar. In fact, they kind of looked like her own. Which was just weird.

"Can I get you something to drink?" Pasting a smile on her face, Alexa shook her head slightly, trying to dislodge the strange sensation creeping down her spine. It wasn't a bad feeling, exactly... just a sense that something here wasn't quite what it seemed.

"I'll order two drinks if you can sit down and talk to me for a minute." The other woman might have looked cranky, but her tone was cautious, careful. As though what she wanted to talk about was something that Alexa might not want to hear.

"I..." It was on the tip of her tongue to refuse, an instinct bred into her by her mother. Nice women just didn't have random discussions with strangers.

"I'm due for a coffee break." Something had her catching her manager's eye and pointing at her watch, signaling that she was taking her break. She was unsettled, wondering what this woman was, but curious too.

As she slid onto the vinyl seat on the other side of the booth, Alexa felt her stomach do a slow roll. Looking at the other woman, she found the redhead scanning her face, as though looking for a reaction.

Apart from the curiosity, Alexa didn't have one to give her. At least, not until the other woman's next words.

"My name is Eleanor Kendrick … Ellie."

Alexa felt her spine stiffen, like she was a puppet and her strings had just drawn her up tight.

"My father was Joseph Kendrick." Ellie continued, and Alexa's gut clenched tight.

"Joseph Kendrick is dead," she said carefully, scanning the other woman's expression.

Ellie flinched. "I wouldn't know anything about that. I don't remember him. But he was my father."

Alexa's mouth opened, then closed. What could she say? Her first reaction was disbelief, because the notion that she had a sister was absolutely absurd.

But Ellie's eyes. They were familiar because, while the color was different, the shape, the fan of long lashes, the heavy lids... they were just like her own.

But her train of thought must have shown on her face, because Ellie placed her hands palm down on the table and leaned in, earnestness replacing the scowl on her pretty face.

"Look. I know this probably sounds like a big crock of shit." Huffing out a breath that made her auburn bangs dance, Ellie worried her lower lip with her teeth. "And I don't have much more information than that to give you. I was cleaning out my—our—my grandmother's attic last summer and I found a box that she'd packed up pretty carefully. It had baby booties, a family picture, and a birth certificate. *Your* birth certificate."

"How did you find me?" Alexa spoke slowly. She'd always believed in Occam's razor—the notion that the most simple of answers was most likely to be the true one.

In this case, that meant that her father, whom she barely remembered, had another child before Alexa. And that her mother either didn't know about said child, or had deliberately not told Alexa about her.

"My husband is the Sheriff in Florence. Do you know Florence? It's about sixty miles from here." Ellie gestured with her hands. "Anyway, that's where we live. Where our grandmother lived. I had him do some digging."

There was an unmistakeable flash of pride on Ellie's face when she spoke about her husband, and Alexa felt a pang in her heart. What must it be like, she wondered, to feel that way about someone? She certainly never had.

"He didn't want me to. Dig, I mean. Said I was asking for trouble." Ellie's eyes met hers then, held, as if asking if her husband had been right.

"What... what do you want?" Alexa formed the words slowly. She wasn't feeling numb, not exactly, but rather as though she was moving in slow motion.

Did this woman want money? Did she know that Alexa's mother came from one of the wealthiest families in the state?

Ellie glared, as if sensing her thoughts, then held out her hands, palms out in a defensive gesture. "I don't want anything from you. We don't need anything. But I thought that we both should know."

Seemingly satisfied with that, Ellie stood, sliding out of the booth.

Alexa, however, was *not* satisfied. She had slid out of the booth too, hurrying after Ellie—after her supposed sister.

*　　*　　*

THAT WAS HOW SHE came to be taking the exit that led into the small town of Florence, Arizona, a place famous—or infamous—for having almost as many inmates as citizens.

Almost as soon as she exited the freeway, Alexa found herself passing one of the massive buildings that housed some of these inmates. Giving in to instinct, she pulled over and looked at the concrete monstrosity.

It was large, several long, interconnected buildings, surrounded by barren yards and a high fence with posted guards. The fence was edged with barbed wire that Alexa would have bet money was also electric, and something about it tickled her memory.

Reaching for the memory, she stared and let her mind whirl. But it was like trying to catch smoke, and finally she let it pass, shrugging and driving on.

Even if she hadn't had GPS, it would have been hard to get lost. The town was small, twenty-five-thousand inhabitants, and Main Street was well marked, full of preserved historic buildings. As she pulled up in front of the motel, one of those wonderfully historic places, she noted that her hands were trembling, a bit.

The barbed wire. It was something to do with that memory that she couldn't quite grasp. Or from the fact that she was about to find answers to questions that she once hadn't even known she'd had.

The motel was constructed of sand colored stucco, and was long and low with an arched entryway. A flag waved in the breeze, the bright red, white and blue, a perfect complement to the pale building.

As Alexa slowly parked, then climbed out of the SUV, she noted that most of the buildings on the street were of a similar construction, and all were clearly very old. It added to the slight sense of disorientation, like she'd entered a different dimension.

Her skin prickled a bit as though someone was watching her, but she quickly shrugged it off. No one in this town knew her. No one was watching her, wondering if she was feeling okay. No one was curious about the accident.

She was just Alexa. She was free.

The air inside the lodgings was surprisingly dry and cool, though heavy with the musty air that came with age. Securing her purse strap over her shoulder, Alexa made her way to the front desk and did her best not to gawk.

Living in Arizona, she'd encountered her fair share of historic places—every elementary school class had done at least one field trip to an old Spanish mission, she was sure of it. But it fascinated her because it was imperfectly perfect in its age, a million years away from the museum like home that she shared with her mother.

It made her feel at home in a way that she rarely had in her life.

"I have a reservation," she said finally, when she stopped staring and arrived at the front desk. Pushing her driver's license across the counter, she blew a wayward strand of hair out of her face. "Under Alexa Kendrick."

The clerk tapped a few keys on an ancient computer, which clunked loudly as it processed.

"Ms. Kendrick has left a message here for you," the clerk said, and Alexa blinked, not sure what he meant until she realized that he was referring to Ellie. "She asked that you go to her work as soon as you can. It's just down the street. I can draw you a map if you'd like to get settled in first."

"No, that's fine, thanks." Alexa wondered why Ellie wanted her there so quickly. She'd planned on taking a bit of time to maybe have a bath and shore up her courage before going to see the woman who just might be her sister.

She still could—no one was making her. But hiding in her room wasn't doing anyone any good either.

"If you'll just point me the right way I'll walk over now." She'd bring her bags in later.

As the clerk had promised, Estelle's Blooms was only two blocks away from the motel, right in the middle of Florence's Main Street. The sign above the door looked like it had once been painted in shades of coral and bright blue, but now was faded to soft pastel tones, a watercolor that helped it blend in with its elderly neighbors. The sign itself might have given an air of neglect to the shop, were it not for the bright front window displays.

Panes of glass so clear it sparkled, framed a stunning riot of blossoms. Since none of them were the orchids her mother cultivated, Alexa had no idea what any of them were—she had most certainly not inherited her mother's green thumb. But the way that they had been arranged, pale pink, stoplight red and crimson on one side and running through a full spectrum...

The sheer visual impact, the beauty, made Alexa's fingers flex, reaching for the paintbrush that wasn't there.

She didn't usually do still life paintings, and rarely painted flowers, but right now she was overwhelmed with the urge to run back to her car and grab her paints.

When had Ellie bought it, she wondered? The age of the sign told her that the shop was not new.

"Oh, you're here!" The bells hanging above the front door jangled as a redheaded tornado whirled through it. "Why are you just standing outside? Come on."

"I just—" Alexa found her arm grasped in slender and surprisingly strong fingers. Momentarily startled out of her ability to speak, she allowed herself to be pulled inside the shop by tugboat Ellie.

She got a brief glimpse at laminate counters, dark green shelves filled with glass vases, and then a ring of keys was being pressed into her hand. Her fingers clenched around it before she frowned and opened her mouth to ask what they were for.

"Here are the keys. The brass one opens the front door here—sometimes it sticks, so make sure to double check it when you close up. And this silver one is for the door that goes upstairs—I haven't been up there in a while so it's probably dusty, but besides that everything should be fine. Make yourself at home." Ellie gathered her hair back with both hands, securing it in a ponytail, as Alexa gaped at her, open mouthed.

"Ellie. Could you maybe explain a bit?" Alexa jangled the

keys that she held. "Like maybe you could tell me why I need these?"

Ellie's forehead wrinkled with exasperation, the same look she'd had when Alexa had first seen her, back at the Boxtree. She was beginning to think that it might be the other woman's perpetual expression.

"What do you mean? I told you in the message I left at the hotel." Looking around distractedly, Ellie reached behind the counter and grabbed a large purse.

"All the message said was to come here as soon as I could," Alexa said slowly, alarm bells starting to shriek in her head. She was all too well acquainted with the signs of being maneuvered into something that she didn't necessarily want. But knowing that still didn't give her much defense against Ellie, who reminded her nothing so much as a steamroller.

"Oh. Well." Ellie slung the purse over her shoulder and, turning to face Alexa, arched an eyebrow.

"My in-laws are snow-birding in Florida. If you can snow-bird when you don't have any snow." Ellie snorted with derision. "Anyway, Gabe's dad had a stroke. Nothing too serious, but his mom's a mess, so we have to go retrieve them. I need someone I can trust to run the shop while we're gone."

Oh, hell no. Alexa had just escaped one trap. She was not about to be led right into another.

"I really don't think—" Alexa started to speak but Ellie was in constant motion, checking the thermostat on the wall, the cash register, something behind the back counter. Alexa exhaled with frustration, finally catching the other woman by the arm, the same way Ellie had her. "Can't you just close the shop?"

Ellie huffed out a laugh, then gestured to the cooler door. Through the glass panes, Alexa could see buckets upon buckets of rainbow blooms.

"I pay a lot of money for my weekly shipment, and it's not like it is inventory that can hold. If I don't sell them, they die, and I take a big loss." Nodding to emphasize her point, she smiled in what Alexa imagined Ellie thought of as an encouraging smile, though it had more than a hint of grimace. "I need someone I trust to run it."

"Surely you have a friend. Someone else," Alexa blurted out. This—this was not what she'd come here for. For a single heart-wrenching moment, Alexa wondered if Ellie had only contacted her because she needed help, but she quickly dismissed the notion.

That would be a lot of trouble to go to, an elaborate story, just to get someone to watch her shop for a few days.

Ellie's face fell in the wake of Alexa's question, just for a single moment before she was again smiling, though the expression was a cold one. "No. No, I really don't have anyone else."

"But you don't even know me!" Frustrated beyond belief, Alex raked her hand through her loose hair. "You don't even know if we're actually related! I'm just a stranger to you!"

Alexa stared when Ellie chuckled, a reaction she hadn't expected.

"Come here." Placing a hand on Alexa's spine, Ellie guided her over to the cooler. In the reflection in the glass, Alexa watched as the other woman tucked her face in close to her own.

Side by side, the familial resemblance was undeniable, even watered down as the reflection was in the glass. Different hair color, different noses and mouths… but the eyes. The curve of the chin, and something about the tilt of the head.

It could have been coincidence, Alexa supposed. But she knew, deep down she knew, that this woman was truly her sister.

It made her all the more desperate not to be left here, alone. She wanted answers. She wanted them now.

"Are you really going to try to tell me that you don't believe we're sisters?" The habitual irritation that Ellie carried melted into a hint of a smile in the translucent reflection. Then flesh and blood Ellie pulled back, turned, and looked Alexa right in the face.

"I'm not sure what I believe anymore." Looking away quickly, Alexa tried to calm herself, even though she was feeling incredibly overwhelmed. "I'm sorry, but I don't."

Her entire body clenched, waiting for Ellie's disapproval— but though she had a hard time speaking her mind, there it was. Alexa didn't know enough about herself anymore, to be able to place trust in anyone else. While her gut was telling her that Ellie was family… well, she just wasn't quite ready to accept that yet.

"Well, I believe it." Ellie didn't sound mad. No, instead there was a definite trace of sympathy in the voice that, if Alexa listened hard enough, was definitely similar to her own. "We're sisters. We're blood, and that means something to me."

"Maybe. But I still really can't— "

"This shop belonged to our grandmother, and so did the apartment upstairs. It's only right that you're the one to watch it."

"Ready to go, babe?" The man who entered, cutting off Alexa's retort, was tall and lean, but there was still no disguising the strength in his body—or the way that he held himself.

Rigid, like a military man. Or, Alexa noted, catching sight of the police cruiser outside, a cop.

He reached out an arm for Ellie who, despite that prickly exterior, cuddled right into it, then turned and pinned Alexa with bright green eyes. "You'd be Alexa, then."

"I… yes." Alexa wasn't typically nervous around cops—she'd always been far too well behaved for that—but nothing about today was typical. And this man, with his deep eyes, looked like he knew things about Alexa that she herself did not.

But in the end, nothing prophetic came out of his mouth. He simply nodded and shook her hand, then herded Ellie out the door. Alexa followed, still protesting that she absolutely couldn't do this, but Ellie talked right over her.

"Ellie. I don't know a damn thing about flowers!" Finally Alexa shouted this as Ellie climbed into the passenger's side of the sheriff's vehicle and rolled down the window. By this point the other woman was distracted by her husband, and just nodded.

"Just sell things. You'll be fine." And then they were gone, the tires kicky up the dry, crumbling asphalt. Not sure what else to do, Alexa watched, speechless, as the car made its way down main street, then turned and drove out of sight.

Alexa wasn't sure how long she stood there, watching as her last life line drove away, wondering what the hell had just happened. She'd arrived in Florence less than an hour ago with a suitcase, a hotel room and a head full of questions. Now she had a flower shop to run, an apartment that be-longed to her supposed grandmother, and even fewer answers than she'd started with.

It was going to be a long few days.

CHAPTER THREE

THE SMALL DINER THAT lay across the street from Estelle's Blooms was about as different from the Boxtree as it could possibly have been. While the restaurant where Alexa waitressed was identical to a thousand other locations across America and therefore rather soulless, the Chat 'n Chew was a different story altogether, tiny and decorated exactly as it had been when it had opened in the mid-fifties.

Alexa was seated in a small booth upholstered in avocado green vinyl, nursing a mug of herbal tea that she didn't particularly like. She was a coffee drinker, but caffeine hadn't seemed like a good idea, not with nerves and anxiety and who knew what else skittering around underneath her skin.

Still somewhat shell shocked by the stunt that the steamroller masquerading as her sister had pulled, Alexa raked her fork through the piece of sweet potato pie that the perky waitress named Alice had brought her. Normally Alexa was hard pressed to meet a sweet that she didn't like, and she'd ordered it thinking that some comfort food might perk her up.

But now it sat on its white plate, railroad tracks from her fork striping the orange goo. Her appetite was just gone.

Since arriving in Florence two hours ago, Alexa had felt a bit like she was walking underwater. She was forced to admit to herself that she'd expected to feel some sort of kinship with the town, some spark of recognition that told her, without a doubt, that this was where her roots were. That here was the place where she would find the answer—the puzzle piece that would fill that empty hole inside of her.

But other than that strange feeling outside of the prison, when she'd seen that barbed wire, there was just a disconcerting lack of... nothing. Just the disappointment that came with Ellie's leaving right away.

There's nothing for you there. Unbidden, her mother's words rang through her mind, and Alexa winced. Truthfully, what had she expected? To stumble across a box that contained the answer to every question she'd ever had about her father, her background?

The nothingness made her panic, a little. What was she doing here, anyway? She was a celebrated artist, and this trip was just postponing her getting back to her life—the life she'd had before the accident.

There was nothing for her here. Her mother had been right. Now she was stuck, prolonging the agony until Ellie got back.

Scowling, she pulled a pen from her purse and, pulling a napkin from the metal dispenser on the table, started to sketch. After she'd inked the first few curves of the waitress' face, she realized with a start that this was the most art that she'd done in a year.

Pausing, Alexa forked up a bite of the pie and scooped it into her mouth. The pure sweetness gave her a jolt, and when she squinted, looked around the small diner, the greyness of her previous thoughts turned to Technicolor brightness and everything suddenly clicked, a sense of rightness.

Maybe she was right where she was supposed to be. For now, anyway.

Grinning to herself, Alexa turned back to her drawing. She finished the sketch of the waitress, then moved on to an elderly woman in a long tie-dyed skirt who sat at the front counter, knitting something large and bright green. She outlined the sign for Estelle's Blooms, visible through the large window of the diner that had yellowed slightly as the years had passed.

Lifting her head, she let her gaze roam the room, searching for her next target. Her eyes landed on a man about her own age, maybe a few years older, and when he lifted his head and looked at her right back, nodding once in acknowledgement, she felt the punch of attraction like a fist in the gut.

He nodded once more, just the slightest jerk of his head, then returned his attention to his meal, but Alexa was left with a surge of adrenaline.

Wow. She'd never felt that kind of instant… *want* before.

She was overcome with the urge to capture it in the only way she knew how.

Stealing surreptitious glances, she pulled a new napkin toward her and began to draw.

The man was seated, of course, but looked like he'd be tall when standing. He looked like he normally filled out his clothing pretty well too, but had recently lost more weight than he could afford to. It stretched the skin a little too tightly over his cheekbones, emphasizing the sharpness of steel grey eyes.

He wore a uniform, navy blue and looking a little bit tired, just like the man. He'd unbuttoned the top two fastenings of the shirt, and had clearly run his fingers through hair that was brown in some lights, and had threads of red in another.

Despite the slight gauntness of his face, he seemed to fill a lot of space. Between that and the uniform, Alexa assumed that he was a prison guard.

As she feverishly sketched, she wondered why on earth she found that so incredibly fascinating.

She continued to draw, stealing glances as he ate what looked to be beans and rice rolled into a tortilla. When her fingers stopped moving, the image done, she found that she herself was starving, and attacked the remains of her pie with a hunger that she hadn't felt in a very long time.

She was swallowing the last bite when the napkin with her drawing suddenly moved, sliding across the table. Slapping a hand down to hold it in place, she jerked her head up and found those dark grey eyes regarding her with cool amusement.

"If you sell that, do I get a cut?"

"Excuse me?" Angry at the intrusion, more than a little embarrassed at being caught, Alexa felt her cheeks flush.

"Relax. I'm just kidding." The man's lips curved up just a hint, the beginnings of a smile. Looking her over carefully, he nodded. "Nice T-shirt."

"Hmm?" Still not sure if she was irritated or not, Alexa looked down at her outfit. Ripped blue jeans, Converse sneakers that had seen better days, and a well-worn T-shirt. The shirt showed the well-known movie poster image from the old cult classic *Jaws*, but in place of the shark was a fluffy little kitten. "Um… thanks."

She wasn't entirely sure if he was making fun of her or not. Now that she was no longer waitressing, she could revert back to what she'd always worn while painting, which, to her mother's dismay, meant jeans and shirts like these—she had an entire collection of them, with a particular fondness with ones for cats. Once in a while she'd even put a blue streak in her hair, just because it felt good.

Or at least, she used to. As she looked up at the stranger and saw that he seemed sincere, she thought that she just might be feeling the urge again.

"Well, I'll leave you to it." The man gave her that little smile again—it was almost as if he'd forgotten how to do a full one, the muscles there but atrophied. His body turned as if to go, and Alexa suddenly found herself pressing the napkin drawing into his hand.

"Here," she blurted, her face flushing again. "You can have it."

Something flickered in his eyes, as though he was puzzled by her actions—no, by being shown some small kindness. It made Alexa's heart ache.

But then he folded the napkin up neatly and tucked it into his shirt pocket. When he looked at her again and this time managed what she'd judge was at least half of a smile, she was pretty sure that the attraction she was feeling was reciprocated.

"Thank you." He looked like he was going to say something else, but didn't, and Alexa found herself disappointed. Just this little bit of flirting—okay, of almost flirting—had made her feel alive. Still, she couldn't help but smile to herself when he rubbed his hand over the pocket where he'd placed her drawing.

She thought he might ask for her number—and she knew she'd give it to him, never mind that romance had been the last thing on her mind for what seemed like forever. That it should probably remain that way until she got back to life as she knew it.

But he didn't ask. He just smiled that strange, sad little smile and walked away—the second time that day that Alexa felt like she'd reached out to someone and they'd left.

Then he was gone, and she didn't even know his name.

*   *   *

ALEXA WAS NOT AN early riser, but the next morning she woke with the sun, feeling as though she'd never fully been asleep, a side effect, she supposed, of the previous day's strange events, coupled with the sounds of an unfamiliar place.

It took a moment for her to remember where she was, and once she did, she closed her eyes, then opened them again, wondering if it was all actually real.

The old-fashioned popcorn ceiling above her head remained the same, as did the pale sunlight filtering in through thin curtains, and the faint musty smell in the air that told her no one had lived in this apartment for some time. Florence. She was in Florence, and yesterday her plans had been turned upside down.

Blinking blearily, Alexa stretched, then tossed back the covers. Padding to the kitchen, she felt that strange sense of someone looking over her shoulder, of intruding someplace she wasn't supposed to be that came with being in an unfamiliar place. Ignoring it, she poked around the small kitchen, looking for a coffee pot.

There wasn't one. Just another fabulous thing to add to a trip that was already going so very well, sarcasm intended. For a long moment she was tempted to just go crawl back under the covers and stay there for the remainder of the day.

She couldn't. She had a flower shop that she had no clue how to open or run.

Irritation settling over her, Alexa slammed a few more cupboard doors until she came across a very battered old metal teakettle. Remembering that she had a package of instant coffee in her purse, she set to work, and within moments had a cup of sweet, steaming caffeine clutched in her hands.

Holding the mug so tightly that it burned her palms, Alexa padded back across the kitchen, down the small hallway and back into the bedroom. There she threw open the curtains and looked out the window at what was early morning in Florence.

Instead of the irritation that she'd expected to double, as she sipped her drink and watched the quiet street, with only the occasional pedestrian or car passing by, Alexa felt a strange sort of peace settle over her, that same feeling she'd gotten the night before, in the diner.

Maybe right here, right now, was where she was supposed to be. If only, she thought wryly, that right now feeling had included the man from the diner the night before.

His face in her mind's eye, her fingers itched for a canvas and her paints. She would love to try to capture those fascinating lines of his cheekbones, his jaw, the exact shade of that russet hair in vivid oil—and after she'd left the diner, she'd cancelled her reservation at the small hotel and retrieved her suitcase and paints, so she could.

If only she didn't have to be downstairs in an hour to open a shop to which she didn't even know how to turn on the cash register.

But as she drained her mug, and let the caffeine settle in her brain, Alexa found that, instead of dreading it, she was actually looking forward to the change in routine. It had been a long time since she'd woken up with any kind of feelings at all about her day—so anxiety, irritation, creativity all filled an emptiness that she she'd been aware of but hadn't quite known how to fill.

The memory drifted in softly as she stepped away from the window, triggered by a flash of buttery yellow sunlight shining through the glass. Just the faintest wisp of knowing, a sense that she'd experienced it sometime before.

A red and white skirt swirled around her legs, which were short and chubby with youth. She sat on the floor here, in this very room, watching the sun as it played through the glass.

"We have to go now, Alexa." Her mother, younger and straighter, face streaked with tears as she scooped Alexa up off the floor. "We have to go home."

"No! Stay! I want to stay here!" Alexa kicked and screamed, reached out for an older woman who crossed her arms over her chest and looked at the floor.

That was it—that was all that she remembered. It left more questions than it answered.

But for Alexa, it was something—one small piece of the puzzle to which she didn't know the design.

And for the moment, it was enough.

Smiling slightly to herself, she pulled a fresh pair of jeans and a T-shirt with a quote from *Star Wars* out of her suitcase, then headed for the bathroom, which, as Ellie had promised, was clean, if a bit dusty.

Today… today she had work to do.

*   *   *

NATE FURY WAS AT the diner again, seated in a booth by the window. Sipping at the thick coffee that was so much better than the sludge in the break room at the prison, he watched the sun rise and waited for his breakfast.

He ate most of his meals here—it was hard to cook on the hot plate at the hotel, not that he was much of a chef at any rate. It was lucky, in fact, that the diner was so close to the hotel, or he'd likely start to skip meals, giving in to the lack of appetite that came hand in hand with the dark cloud of depression that had surrounded him for so long.

It would have been so easy to slip back into that welcoming darkness, a battle he fought daily. But some small part of him, somewhere deep down, understood that this was important—going through the motions of life, even when you didn't feel alive.

So he stopped at the Chat n' Chew for a meal on his way to the prison, and again when he left. Not quite three square meals a day, but far better than he'd done in the days and months before he'd come to Florence.

As his breakfast was delivered, he settled back in the booth and looked through the pane of glass, happy that his shift was over. They'd gotten a new transfer in the night before, a young man who had managed to get under Nate's skin in a way that few did. But even after years as a cop, this one... rather than denying his crime, as most did, he'd told Nate about it, first thing. Had been proud, as he'd recounted details that had made Nate sick.

Normally the inmates didn't bother him—he'd seen it all, working the beat in Los Angeles. But this one? He'd made Nate think about true evil, had reminded Nate of the reasons that he'd left the force and taken the job in Florence in the first place. Reasons that had led him to stop eating and to start drinking.

The arrival of his breakfast broke through the thirst that made its presence known whenever Nate dwelled too long on what had been, and he forced himself to focus on the simple act of lifting food to his mouth, of chewing and swallowing. He'd ordered *huevos rancheros* again, hold the meat—he'd been vegetarian since his early days on the police force, when he'd spent some time breaking up illegal dog fighting rings. It hadn't been much of a stretch to go from feeling sick over the pain of the pit bulls to not feeling too comfortable with the ways in which meat went from animal to Styrofoam packet at the supermarket.

As he ate, a flash of color from across the street caught his eye. Sipping at his coffee, he turned his head to find the woman he'd met here in the diner last night, standing in the doorway of Estelle's Blooms across the street, looking more than a little bit lost.

That was odd. He kept to himself as much as he could, but he'd been pretty sure that the woman who worked at that shop had red hair. Not that it was a permanent thing with women, of course, but he was also pretty sure that the redheaded woman was married to the Sheriff. The woman he'd met last night had had no ring on her finger, and the punch of heat that had passed between them when their eyes had met hadn't seemed like it had belonged to a married woman, either.

Curiosity and all, Nate probably would have left well enough alone, content to keep to himself and watch a pretty woman on a pretty morning. But when she started dragging plain white buckets out in front of the shop and filling them with rainbow colored blooms, he found that his fingers itched to touch.

Something about this woman pulled at him. A curious thing, that she was able to penetrate the darkness that had surrounded him for so long.

As he watched, the woman started to arrange the flowers in the buckets. He wasn't sure what, exactly, she was expecting with the meticulous way she was organizing the blooms, but he couldn't hold back his laugh when she stomped her foot with frustration, the movement animating her entire body, when the flowers clearly didn't do what she wanted them to.

Pushing away his empty plate and signing the receipt that would put the meal on his account, Nate pushed himself away from the table, and headed across the street.

This strange woman was a ray of light that had managed to break through the gloom that he never seemed quite able to shake, at least not anymore.

Because of that, he wasn't quite ready to let go.

CHAPTER FOUR

NATE FOLLOWED HIS INSTINCTS and found himself outside of the diner. It was still morning, but already the heat of the Arizona day had worked on the tar in the street, and it sucked at his shoes, making him work harder for every step.

Alexa was intent on her work, and he took the time that she was unaware of his presence to examine her in more detail than he'd been able to the previous night. On the shorter side of things, but with some very appealing curves that looked like they might fit a man's hands nicely. Her hair was long, reaching to her shoulder blades even pulled back as it was. The way the pale morning lit hit it highlighted the maple sugar color, as well as her pale skin, smooth and clear without any of that gook that women sometimes wore.

When she cursed and turned, pale eyes widening at the sight of him, he felt that sizzle that came with a strong attraction. Yes, he thought, a beautiful woman, who didn't have the slightest idea that she was.

"Um. Hi." Having once been a cop meant that he instinctively noted down details, body language. Right now he noticed that, while the woman fidgeted and tucked a stray wisp of her hair behind her ear, something that usually told him the person was out of their element, she met his stare head on. Contradictory, and fascinating.

And… there was something about her. Something that made him wonder if he'd maybe met her before. Or at least seen her somewhere.

"You're the guy from last night." The woman arched her back, and Nate felt more pleased than he should have when a hint of pleasure flickered over her pretty face. And if he also noted the way the movement pressed nice, full breasts against the thin cotton of her T-shirt, well, he was a man, after all.

He nodded, trying to tear his gaze away from her so that he didn't come off as creepy. When she shifted her weight from foot to foot, he wasn't entirely sure that he'd managed.

"Can I help you with something?" Her words came out with a little more force than they could have, and Nate couldn't help but smile. Two socially awkward humans, trying to decide if they wanted a flirtation. If they weren't careful, this would quickly devolve into an episode of *The Big Bang Theory*.

"I need some flowers." Nate said the first thing that came out of his mouth, then winced. *Way to be original, Fury. Bet no one's said that to her before.*

But to her credit, the woman just nodded. "Anything particular in mind?" With a jerk of her head indicating that he should follow her inside, she stooped to prop open the glass door with a large grey brick, then entered the shop.

"I'll take whatever you think is pretty." Nate followed her in, not above taking a surreptitious look at the sweet curves of her backside as he did. He'd been so depressed for so many months, and attraction of any kind hadn't been able to fight its way through the dark.

But this woman? Something about her was different.

"Okay." The woman exhaled loudly, and Nate thought she looked relieved, which puzzled him a bit. The confusion only thickened as he watched her move around the shop.

She just didn't seem very comfortable in her surroundings, opening three drawers before locating a pair of clippers, and bumping her curvy hips on the edge of the counter, the garbage can, the cash register every time she turned around. More than that, every bloom that she picked up was held gingerly between thumb and forefinger, as if she didn't have a clue what to do with it and more, was maybe a little bit nervous.

Fascinated, he watched as she worked. Like she'd done outside, she spent an inordinate amount of time comparing colors, even muttering to herself as she worked. But when it came to arranging the stems together, she was clumsy and awkward, finally cursing under her breath and jamming the mass of green together.

"Christ," she muttered to herself as she held the bouquet up in front of her and surveyed her handiwork. Nate felt his lips twitch and struggled to hold back a smile when she stomped toward the front counter and held out her creation with a huff of her breath.

What was her story? Why was she here? He was dying to know.

It wasn't his business. Part of why he'd changed jobs was to surround himself with anonymity. Caring led to pain, and he'd had enough of that for a lifetime.

"How much?" He pulled his wallet from his pants pocket. She raised her eyebrows at him.

"I can't charge you for this." Together they surveyed the undeniably ugly bouquet.

Some of the stems were broken, and twisted at awkward angles. The rest of the stems had been forced together so tightly that Nate felt his own lungs quiver for breath in response. The heads of the blossoms... they'd been packed together like sardines in a tin can, one giant ball that did nothing to emphasize each flower's delicate beauty.

"It's not that bad." He felt his mouth curl into a half smile—he had a hard time managing a full one these days, though right now he was close.

The woman's eyes met his over the top of the bouquet, and they were full of disbelief. He couldn't help it—he barked out a short laugh.

"No, really. The colors are nice." And they were—the time she'd taken over that had paid off, the big ball of blooms' only saving grace. "I'm happy to pay for them."

Anything to make her smile, though why he felt the driving need, he wasn't entirely sure. More than the desire to see her face light up, Nate felt that intense curiosity, which he finally gave in to.

"So, what's your story?" Her head snapped up, and he knew he'd been blunt. He couldn't help it—it was just how he was. But he did curse a bit internally as he warned himself not to scare her away.

"I beg your pardon?" Wariness shadowed her face as she thrust the bouquet into his hands and stepped back, crossing her arms over her chest. Classic defensive body language.

Well, in for a penny. "You clearly don't know your way around. I've never seen you before. Did you just move to town?"

His eyes met hers, noted the suspicion in hers. "Are you a cop or something?"

"Would it matter if I was?" He knew he couldn't read too much into her defensiveness, though something about her was setting a quiet alarm ringing in his head—some people were just naturally skittish around law enforcement.

"Would it matter if I cared?" She countered, raising her chin and not backing down. Nate liked that spark of spirit, and the way it broke through the haze of grey that had surrounded him for so long.

With another half-smile, he held his hands up, palms out. "Not a cop. Just interested."

Just interested. What did he mean by that, exactly? He was breaking his anonymity rule here.

But something about her just wouldn't let him leave it alone.

She broke his stare, studying the bouquet intently as she studiously tried to rearrange one of the stems. He was certain that she was dodging the question, and was trying to think of something to say to get them both out of the awkward mess, when she lifted her head and pinned him with that intent stare of hers, the one that said not only was she observing, but she was *seeing*.

"I'm watching the shop for a few days. For my… sister." She stumbled over the last word, and though Nate wanted to know why, he told himself he'd done quite enough pushing already.

He opened his mouth; to say what, he wasn't sure. But then she shook her head, as if to shake herself out of her uncertainty, and looked up at him through the thick tangle of mink colored lashes.

Something in that look hit him square in the chest. It was something more than her looks, though she was an undeniably attractive woman. But this—this was some connection. One of those indescribable instances in which two people are pulled together, and nothing they do can stop it.

He said none of this, though, retreating instead into the stoicism in which he was the most comfortable.

The silence between them hung heavily in the air, pregnant with unspoken words.

"Who are the flowers for?" She spoke first—Christ, he didn't even know her name.

He hadn't intended to buy flowers at all, let thought far enough ahead to decide on a recipient, so he went with his kneejerk response.

"They're for you." As he spoke he felt that high that went hand in hand with flirtation, though he hadn't planned to hit on her when he'd walked across the street. He'd just... he'd been pulled. As if by an invisible hand.

It wasn't fair to this woman. He was a mess. He was in no place to be starting something.

Yet a little voice whispered in his head—*haven't you suffered enough?*

He watched as her eyes lit with surprise, and a shy smile curved her lips, which only enhanced her appeal.

"I—" She ran a tongue over her lower lip. "I'm Alexa."

"Nate." He thought about holding out a hand, but shaking was not what he wanted to do with this woman.

How very much he wanted it unnerved the hell out of

him. And just like that, the interior of the tiny flower shop started to feel a little bit too small, the walls threatening to close in on him.

If he didn't leave before that happened, he knew from experience that he could find himself shrouded in darkness. He didn't want this woman—*Alexa*—to see him like that.

He also didn't want to be the head case who ran out of her shop for no reason, either. Strangely enough, looking into those wide, shining eyes of hers was like a cool balm on the agitated energy of his soul.

"I'll see you around, Alexa." Her little smile carried him out the door, where he sucked in air until he got lightheaded.

He was tired. This was nothing new. But the little bit of lightness in his heart that carried him home?

That definitely was, and he wanted more.

*   *   *

ALEXA KNEW IT WAS foolish, but she used her limited skills to arrange the bouquet of flowers in a cheap glass vase on the counter of the shop. They still seemed ridiculously messy to her artistic eye, but something about the time spent with the blooms, touching the silky petals, inhaling the sweet scent, satisfied her in a way that only painting ever had.

Maybe it wasn't the arranging, but the fact that the flowers had been given to her by the handsome, brooding man who'd seemed like he'd stepped right out of the pages of a romance novel.

"Down, girl." Alexa whispered to herself as her heart did a pleasant little flip. She wasn't really in any place to be starting something. She didn't even live here, didn't know how long she'd stay.

But if it gave her joy, and didn't hurt anyone, then what was wrong with savoring the sweet rush? It had been so long since she'd felt these exciting little shivers.

Humming to herself, Alexa spent the next few hours exploring the shop that had belonged to—it was hard to say it— her grandmother. She was an artist, yes, but she wasn't the stereotypically messy, absent minded type, and she didn't like not knowing where things were, not feeling comfortable in her surroundings. So she memorized the whereabouts of tools that she didn't have a clue as to the use of, and different kinds of ribbons and raffia, and the extra rolls of paper for the cash register. The till itself required a great deal of poking at before it would do anything, and not a little bit of frustration when customers came in before she'd figured it out. But she still didn't feel comfortable charging for her ugly bouquets anyway, and she figured that Ellie was just going to have to eat the lost profit in return for giving Alexa so little information before she'd taken off.

Alexa was standing in the cooler, flipping through a massive hard covered floral dictionary and comparing the pictures to the blooms in front of her, when the bell above the door chimed yet again. It wasn't in her nature to be surly, not like it seemed like Ellie habitually was but Alexa was an introvert. There was a reason she'd chosen a solitary career.

Too many people, even one by one, grated on her. So she forced a smile over gritted teeth as she pushed out of the cooler to greet the petite, white haired woman who'd entered the shop.

"Good afternoon." Her voice sounded much cheerier than she felt—at least, she hoped it did, because the high from her encounter with Nate had faded, leaving her more than a little overwhelmed. "May I help you with anything?"

The woman had sparkly lavender rimmed glasses on a beaded chain around her neck; when she saw Alexa she used gnarled fingers to put them on scowling as she focused in.

"Who are you, then?" The way she looked at Alexa made her squirm as though she'd done something bad enough to earn a detention. In fact, she wouldn't have been at all surprised to find that this woman had been a teacher before her golden years hit.

"I'm Alexa." She forced herself to take a deep breath and smile, though inside her head she was screaming. Done, done, she was so done. And she was supposed to deal with the public for a few *days?*

If Ellie would just come home, Alexa would never feel uninspired to paint again.

"I didn't ask your name, girlie. I asked who you were." The older woman glared, as if Alexa really should have understood that right off the bat.

Alexa *wanted* to tell the woman that it was none of her business, and it was on the tip of her tongue to do just that. Something held her back.

"I'm a—I'm a friend of Ellie's." Why she didn't claim Ellie as her sister to this woman, when she had to Nate, she didn't know. Though she'd known him for less than a day, the man had nestled himself into a subset in her mind—he was just different from everyone else.

The woman glared over the top of her glasses—or at least,

Alexa thought she did, but it was hard to tell, with all the wrinkles that folded the paper thin skin.

"I've got eyes, girlie. You're the other child. Estelle's other granddaughter." Sniffing, never doubting that she was right, the woman gestured to a bucket of—Alexa was pretty sure they were carnations—that she'd arranged in a bucket on the counter. "Those on special?"

"Everything's on special," Alexa replied, smirking a bit inside—it was her small way of exacting revenge for Ellie dumping this entire situation in her lap. But as she spoke she looked her customer over cautiously, hooked by the woman's words.

The other child.

"Hmpf. You're a sight less tight fisted than your sister, then." The woman nodded approvingly, then used her cane to drag the bucket down the counter to where she stood, because clearly, she couldn't lower herself to walk there herself. Water splashed onto the counter, soaking the shoulder of Alexa's T-shirt, but she barely noticed.

"Sister." She swallowed thickly. How would this woman know that she had a sister when she was even convinced herself? "How do you—"

"Mrs. Robert Gunderson. Lived next door for fifty years." The woman jerked a thumb at herself before pulling a bundle of red carnations out of the bucket, the movement causing the sweetly spicy scent to fill the air. Out of their container, the paper that Alexa had wrapped them in was clearly soaked, two large lumps breaking off to plop wetly on the counter as they stood there. "You're supposed to wrap these in plastic, girlie. Cellophane."

Alexa should have been frustrated with her error—only an idiot wouldn't realize that paper would get soaked in the water in the buckets, after all. But she found it hard to care, when she was suddenly consumed by one thought, one little thing that froze her in place.

This woman might have known her father.

She opened her mouth to ask, slightly afraid that if she managed to get even a single word out, they would *all* come tumbling forth in a never ending stream, but the woman held up her hand, halting the verbal diarrhea before it could start.

"It's not my place to tell you about your sister. Assuming I knew. Which I probably don't," the woman said in a quiet voice that belied her prickly exterior, and Alexa thought she saw something like understanding flash through the other woman's eyes. "But I remember you."

Before Alexa could even process that life changing statement, the lavender glasses were off the crooked nose, the flowers tucked in the crook of Mrs. Gunderson's arm, soggy paper and all. "See that you don't make any noise after seven. I go to bed early."

Then the woman was gone, the bells chiming merrily as she shoved her way through the door. Alexa was left alone with more questions than answers.

It wasn't until she closed up the shop for the night that she realized Mrs. Gunderson hadn't even paid for her flowers.

CHAPTER FIVE

A LEXA'S CELL PHONE RANG as she set up the small portable easel and a fresh canvas on the tiny balcony of the apartment over Estelle's Blooms. The theme music from *Jaws* blared in the scorching evening air, announcing that it was her mother on the other end of the line, and though she was ashamed of the thought, for a split second Alexa considered letting the call go through to voice mail.

She didn't like keeping secrets, especially not from her mother, with whom she told almost everything. But a little voice in her head was holding her back from spilling everything.

"Mom." Telling herself not to be ridiculous, Alexa finally snatched up her phone and accepted the call.

She was not going to avoid her own mother. Even if part of her was wondering if her mother could possibly have known about this secret sister situation.

"Hello, Alexa." To some, Tracy might sound cool, but Alexa knew that was just her mother's way—she wasn't given to grand emotional gestures. "It's good to hear your voice. I thought you might have called when you got in."

"I'm sorry." The words were said automatically, even as a trickle of anger broke through. Lord, but she was tired of these little guilt trips. "I was a bit... overwhelmed... when I arrived."

"Don't tell me you're remembering things?" Her mother's voice hurt her ears, more forcefully than the other woman usually spoke, and Alexa winced.

"Ow. No, Mom. Not really." Tucking the phone between her shoulder and cheek, Alexa began to set out her tubes of paints, savoring the familiar but long missed surge of joy that never failed to appear when she sorted through the rainbow of colors. "Well..."

"What?" Once again, her mother sounded more *intense* than she usually did. "What's happened?"

"Are you all right, Mom?" Alexa really wasn't sure what to make of this. Tracy Cunningham just didn't *do* excitable. "You sound a little... off."

"I'm fine," Tracy snapped, and Alexa blinked in surprise, but before she could reply, Tracy continued, sucking in an audible breath. "I'm just... worried. That's all. Worried about you away from home, after everything that happened."

"Oh, Mom." As she so often was with her mother, Alexa felt torn. She loved her mother, absolutely she did. And she didn't want to cause her any distress.

But she was also an adult, something Tracy had a very hard time remembering. It seemed extreme, but Alexa suspected that if she gave the okay, her mother would have her live back home forever.

The overprotectiveness came, Alexa knew, from an overly enhanced fear that harm would come to her, and the accident

51

certainly hadn't helped that. But Alexa wanted—needed—to move on.

She couldn't with her mother trying so desperately to wrap her in a cocoon.

"The accident was a year ago, Mom," Alexa reminded her mother gently, wincing a bit as she waited for the inevitable sarcasm meant to put her in her place. "We have to move on sometime."

There was a long silence, during which each listened to the other breathing. Then...

"I just don't know if I'm ready." Tracy whispered so very quietly that Alexa wasn't sure she heard her correctly. When she decided she had, she was so shocked that she blurted out the first thing in her mind.

"I had a hard time driving into town. Outside one of the prisons." She heard her mother suck in a breath, but pushed forward, her own voice loud and unfiltered. "There were the-se... these big long stretches of barbed wire. I don't know if it was a memory, exactly. But it creeped me out."

"Alexa," her mother breathed into the phone, sounding every bit as shocked as she likely was. "I do *not* want you spending time near the prisons. Do you hear me?"

"Excuse me?" Irritation percolated just beneath her skin. "What I do with my time here is my own business."

Damn it, but what was it about her mother that made her feel—and act—sixteen again? She could have alleviated Tracy's concerns, could have told her that she wasn't near the prison at all. Instead, she felt the need to stomp her foot and declare her independence.

There was silence for what felt like an hour but was probably only thirty seconds. Alexa balanced on the tightrope that de-fined her relationship with Tracy, but her mother spoke before she could decide which side to fall off on.

"I'm sorry." Her mother's voice was harsh, and Alexa felt her mouth fall open, just a bit.

Her mother rarely apologized. In fact, Alexa could proba-bly count on one hand the number of times she remembered it happening in her life.

"Mom, I—" But the other woman cut her off.

"Are you feeling like painting at all yet?" Tracy continued as though the last minute of conversation hadn't happened, and since Alexa didn't much feel like delving into anything either, she followed her mother's lead.

"I was just setting them up, right now." She couldn't help but smile a bit—it felt so damn *good*, just to run her fingers over the blank canvas in front of her.

"That's wonderful, Alexa." And her mother truly sounded like she meant it. "What are you going to paint?"

"A view of the prison." The words left Alexa's mouth un-bidden, but she instantly recognized them as true. She'd intended to paint a landscape, some of the mountains and desert that were visible here, on the edge of town. But as she surveyed her view, she realized that the prison-scape was, in fact, what was catching her artist's eye.

"I don't understand why you would joke about something like that," her mother snapped in return, and Alexa felt her spine stiffen. "I don't like this. I don't like it at all."

Again, the harshness was surprising. Because it was so out of character, Alexa held her tongue against the surge of angry words that threatened to overflow.

"I hated that town," Tracy said finally, her tone suddenly weary, alarming Alexa further. "I've always hated it. Please come home soon."

Then her mother hung up, again something quite out of character. Alexa was left staring down at the dead line in her hand, wondering what had just happened.

Likely her mother really was acting out because of her unease over Alexa being away from home after the accident. That was logical. Rational.

Yet, when Alexa turned back to her blank canvas, to the paints that held so much potential joy, she couldn't deny that the entire conversation had made her very, very uneasy.

*   *   *

THE UNSETTLING CONVERSATION WITH her mother had left Alexa both confused and a little bit manic. She often felt the latter when she was entering a period of deep creativity. It satisfied a starving part of her soul when she was able to sit on the small balcony and channel the energy into art, her fingers creating a slightly abstract silhouette of one of the prisons in the distance, with a band of barbed wire stretching across the foreground of the canvas as the focal point. It was decidedly darker than anything she'd ever painted before, but it truly represented where she was in her life at that moment.

After the need to paint had eased, Alexa had been left with a different kind of urgency—an urge she hadn't been able to ignore, the need to find something, anything that proved without a doubt that she was who Ellie said she was. A starting point to research her past from.

She still didn't understand why, but she knew, she just knew, that if that one mystery was solved, she'd be better able to lay to rest the blankness of her car accident—she'd have built a solid foundation on which to stand through the uncertainty.

That determination was the only thing that carried her up into the hard to access, dim attic that made up the very top of the building that housed the flower shop and the apartment. As the sun sank lower in the sky—early evening by the time Alexa packed up her easel—she wished that she'd thought to come up here earlier.

She could go back down into the apartment. There was nothing that said she had to do this exploring now. Or even that she had to explore at all.

"Yes, I do." Alexa ignored the fact that she was talking to herself, rationalizing that she wasn't crazy until she started answering her own questions. Frowning at her own thoughts, she pushed forward through the dust.

The small space was half organized, one side neatly lined with symmetrical plastic tubs. The other was jammed with cardboard boxes of varying shapes and sizes, some sealed, some torn open and half empty.

A quick survey told Alexa that most of those cardboard boxes contained items of little interest—vintage Tupperware going yellow with age, clothing that spanned fashion of several decades and smelled of mothballs, tangled Christmas lights and glass tree decorations.

Her heart sank as she looked.

Ellie had made mention of finding Alexa's birth certificate in Estelle's attic. Alexa knew that part of her had hoped it would still be here—or more, other parts of her hidden past, ones that Ellie hadn't yet come across.

"Ugh." Settling back on her heels, Alexa ran a hand through her hair with frustration. It was getting harder to see, and nothing of interest was jumping out at her.

Maybe because they didn't exist. Maybe because this attic now held nothing more interesting than the remnants of the life of an old woman she hadn't known. After the strange conversation with Mrs. Gunderson, Alexa was pretty sure that woman was in fact her grandmother, but for all intents and purposes, she was still a stranger. A stranger wasn't likely to give Alexa any clues to... anything.

The small circular window was the only source of rapidly dwindling light, and the bars that crossed through it, combined with the angle of the light slanting in, created a massive, shadowy X on the far wall of the attic. Alexa felt her gaze drawn to that exact place, the shadows marking the spot—though what spot, she had no idea.

She followed the footprints through the thick dust that covered the floor, judging by their size that they belonged to Ellie. Here, where she hadn't looked before, was a smaller cardboard box that she hadn't noticed before, the top carefully folded closed.

Alexa's heart leapt. This. Yes, this. She just had a feeling that it was going to yield something that would change her life.

Carefully she knelt down, slid her fingers beneath the flaps and eased the box open.

It was empty. Completely empty.

"Shit." Pinching her lips together, Alexa tried to get a grip on an unexplained tidal wave of emotions. Her mother had always encouraged control.

She couldn't. The last few days—it had all been too much. So she slammed her fist into the wall, savoured the brightness of the bite of pain, and did it again. And again.

"Shit. Shit. Shit!" She didn't know who she was anymore, and it looked like she wasn't about to. In that moment she understood why it was so vitally important to her that she understand more about her father, about the people she came from.

Not being able to remember a tragic event that had almost killed her—it had managed to steal some part of her identity, the security of knowing who she was a person.

She'd given up hope of remembering the accident—and wasn't entirely sure that she wanted to, at any rate—but understanding all of this, this that had been kept secret from her?

She thought that it might help to fill that hole inside of her, the one that almost dying had torn open. And that explained her absolutely bitter disappointment at not finding anything, not one single scrap of information that she could use as filler in that gaping chasm.

"Damn it all to hell!" Alexa thumped her fist against the wall one last time, wincing, knowing that the flesh was going to bruise.

From somewhere above dropped a leather bound book. It flopped gracelessly to the ground at her side, its impact raising a cloud of dust that made Alexa cough even as she let out a small shriek and jumped, clutching her hand to her chest.

Looking up, in the direction the thing had fallen from, she noted a rafter arching above—the book must have been sitting on the plank of wood. She frowned down at the book.

Odd place to keep something like that. Especially if it had been Estelle's. In her experience, the elderly weren't much given to climbing around like monkeys to store things.

But... maybe this was that *thing* she'd been searching for so desperately? A folder holding her birth certificate? A photo album?

Pulse accelerating, Alexa cautiously picked up the book and studied the outside—not real leather, like she'd thought, but vinyl of some kind. A skinny, generic looking binder with a slender piece of twine wrapped around it like a present.

Her heart thudded in her chest as she unwrapped that piece of twine. She ignored it and turned back the black cover.

The binder was jammed full of photocopied pages, single sided and haphazardly hole punched. The pages were crammed with spiky, blocky printing that Alexa had to squint to read. One line jumped out at her, and when she read it, then re-read it, certain she'd misunderstood, she felt a sickly spike of adrenaline surge through her flesh.

I've been watching her.

"No." Heart pounding, she slammed the book shut, though even she thought that the reaction was a little bit extreme. But that one line—those four words—made her feel ever so faintly sick.

"Don't be ridiculous." Alexa chided herself, fingers clutched tight on the book. It was just that—just a book. She didn't even know yet if it had anything to do with her family, her background.

Gritting her teeth, she opened the book, again settling on the first page, searching for the line that had made her jump.

The words that surrounded it didn't make any sense.

My whole life, I've wondered what it would be like to have complete control over someone. To hold their life in my hands, mine to command, to control.

I don't want to wait any longer... but I've waited long enough that it has to be perfect. And I've chosen the one that I want.

I've been watching her. And she doesn't know.

"What is this?" Alexa sank back on her heels, her muscles stiff with tension, making her movements jerky and awkward.

This... well, it could be anything. But the fact that it had been hidden in Estelle's attic—in Ellie's attic—gave Alexa a very, very bad feeling.

An echo of some memory chose that moment to waft its tendrils into her mind. Nothing concrete—and image of a woman, overlain with that barbed wire. Like she'd read about something like that in the paper, and this... journal... or whatever it was, had somehow connected to that distant thought.

It creeped her right the hell out. She'd been searching for something, but this wasn't it. Those few line she'd read... she didn't think she wanted to read anymore.

Alexa sat still for a few minutes, the book lying open in her lap, the lines she'd read seeming to float above the page.

The wisps wouldn't leave her alone, grabbing at her until she felt sick.

That made up her mind. It didn't matter why this book was here, in this attic.

She wanted nothing more to do with it. And so she dragged over a folding ladder, climbed up to the top. Stretched to her full height, and replaced the book on the beam from which it had fell.

It was none of her business. So she was going to pretend that she'd never found it at all.

CHAPTER SIX

NATE WOKE UP WITH his heart hammering against his rib cage, cold sweat drenching the sheets, and a raging thirst that water wouldn't quench.

Sucking in great ragged breaths, he stared up at the ceiling and tried to will his pulse to slow. Reminding himself that reaching for a bottle would only make him feel worse, no matter how clawing the need.

Closing his eyes again, he let his heavy frame sink down into the mattress. It was lumpy, not very comfortable, but he hadn't expected much more from the cheap motel where he'd chosen to live.

It wasn't that he couldn't afford something better, a nice apartment or even a small house. He knew, deep down he knew, that he stayed here because he felt like he didn't deserve more.

Worse? It was the truth.

The early morning light shining through the crack in the ugly patterned curtains was painfully bright, insisting on dispelling the darkness when every last part of him wanted to wallow in it. To let it twine its arms around him and pull him down, down into a place from which we would never climb out.

The alcohol would help him with that—would add its welcoming weight and help him sink so far that he might never come back. Every time it happened, the depression descending, it was harder and harder to remember to live.

The darkness was seductive. It was a daily battle to not have a bottle of whiskey sitting on his bedside table each day. He'd never considered himself an alcoholic, not really, but he'd scared himself enough to cut alcohol from his life, aware that it was making him worse and that the end of the day, he wasn't the one who'd died.

The reminder was enough to have him rolling over to his side, though the movement took way more energy than it should have.

This was the decisive moment, the one that always came. Did he pull it together, try to stumble his way out of the grey? Or did he just close his eyes and let it all go?

Shifting his weight, he stared aimlessly at the battered alarm clock that sat on the cheap bedside table. The red, blinking numbers told him that he needed to get up, get moving, but no matter what his brain commanded, his body was heavy as stone.

This, his hotel room, his job at the prison, the entire town, it all seemed like some kind of hallucination. Like he'd wake up and find himself back in Los Angeles, back in the job that had so drastically changed his life.

What was that bit of white sticking out from behind the clock? He squinted, tried to make it out, and finally remembered.

The other night, when he'd first met Alexa, he'd placed the white napkin with her sketch of him on the bedside table, where he could easily see it.

He liked looking at it, not because he wanted to admire himself, or anything, but because it had been drawn by her hand. It contained some of the brightness that drew him to her.

This morning, that drawing was what gave him the strength to prop himself up on his elbows, then to draw himself up to a sitting position, the sheets pooling at his waist. Shaking his head, feeling the brush of the russet colored hair on the skin of his forehead, he reached for the drawing.

This woman, the one who had put a bit of her soul into this little sketch—she wasn't perfect either. His every instinct said that she had secrets, and yet… and yet none of this darkness clung to her, like it did to him.

Maybe that was part of his attraction to her—his shadows to her light. No matter what the reason, he knew he wasn't going to be strong enough to do what he should, namely, pull away from her so that he didn't bring her down.

No… he needed that brightness. Craved it.

Thinking of Alexa, of maybe stopping by to see her, was what finally drew him from bed. Untangling the sheets from where they had twined around him during a restless night, he finally, finally sat up, planted his feet on the scratchy carpet. Stood, wobbling only a little before striding naked across the room to the bathroom.

He didn't bother to look in the mirror—he knew what he'd see. A face that was thinner than it should have been, and eyes with dark smudges beneath them. But the cold water that he turned on full got his blood moving, and he knew that when he got out of the shower he at least wouldn't be so pale.

"Aah." When he couldn't stand it anymore, Nate added a twist of the hot water faucet to the cold. His skin screamed at him for the abrupt temperature change, but uncomfortable as it was, it cleared the lingering fog from his head.

Allowed him to remember what had caused him to go to bed with his emotions even, but slide into depression overnight.

He'd had the nightmare again. The one that would never leave him, because it was real. Not something that he'd manufactured in his brain, but a memory, a mental snapshot of blood and bitter cold.

Nate. Watch out!

The smell of blood in his nostrils as Nate turned, was able to avoid being shot himself, as Jud had been. The rattle of his partner's breath as Nate took precious moments to subdue their attacker, a kid barely out of high school who'd gotten desperate at the first wail of sirens.

An armed robbery gone wrong. So wrong, that by the time Nate had the perp secured, lying face down on the concrete, Jud's eyes had been glazed over, his soul already on its way home.

His partner had been steps ahead of him in that alleyway because Nate had been nursing a sore ankle, his own fault for leaving free weights on the floor to trip over in the middle of the night. Something seemingly so inconsequential.

But because Nate hadn't put away those fucking weights after his workout, Jud had gotten into the alley first. Jud had cornered the panicked kid, and Jud had been shot, straight through the stomach, a wound that there was no coming back from.

It should have been me.

Nate had friends, and his parents were alive, but there was no one who depended on him ultimately—no one whose life would fall apart if he'd been the one to die.

Jud? Jud had a wife and two children, a six year old boy and a four year old girl. An entire family whose lives were torn to shreds.

Yes, it should have been him. But instead he was here, caught in not hell, but purgatory. Forced to put one foot in front of the other, day after never-ending day. No sun to burn away the clouds—and he didn't *want* the light.

He didn't deserve it.

But since meeting Alexa… he craved it.

*   *   *

HE FOUND ALEXA SITTING on a wobbly looking stool in front of the flower shop. A large pad of bound paper was open in her lap, and a hand holding a pencil was sketching furiously on the snowy white paper.

She was so absorbed in what she was doing that she didn't look up as he approached, though the change in the angle of her body told him that she knew he was there. Stuffing his hands in the pockets of his uniform pants, he waited, patiently, until finally her hand slowed and she looked up at him with those wide, expressive eyes.

"Hi." Her skin was pale, and there were violet shadows underneath them. The urge to make everything better in her world didn't make any sense at all—he barely knew her. But the feeling lifted him up out of the clinging dregs of nightmare and depression, and he hadn't nearly enough of those moments lately not to reach for it with both hands and hold on tight.

"May I look?" He gestured at her notepad. She studied him silently, then tilted the paper so that he could see it.

She'd been sketching a book. It was a simple image, dark covers surrounding a stack of paper, bound with some kind of cord—a journal, perhaps.

But something about the way she'd drawn it—maybe the fact that she'd taken the time to shade the entire background, adding darkness—it made ghostly fingers play over the base of his spine.

"What's that?" Even when he shifted his attention from the art back to her face, he found that he could still see it in his mind's eye, burned into his mind.

"I don't know, exactly." Alexa let out a short, startled laugh, standing then stretching. The movement caused her breasts to be outlined by her T-shirt, and though his libido had been rather firmly on hold through his depression, the sight of that soft flesh had fire roaring back to life, licking along his skin.

"I don't know much of anything anymore," she continued, shifting a step closer to him. When her eyes locked on his own, something snapped tight between them, a connection he hadn't asked for and couldn't help.

There was more than a little fear in those amazing eyes, too—though whether it was of him or of something else, he had no way of knowing. All he understood in that moment was that something about this woman made him want to move heaven and earth to make her happy. To keep her safe.

"You don't have to be afraid of me." His voice was low and his words sounded raw. "Or of anything else. I swear."

"I believe you." He took in the way her lower lip trembled, the almost innocent lines of her painfully beautiful face.

Then, as though he had absolutely no say in the matter whatsoever, his hands were gently cupping Alexa's cheeks. He heard her soft intake of breath, his own quiet moan as he brushed his thumbs over the smooth planes of her jaw.

He was going to kiss her. He just might die if he didn't. And though he had no idea of how he would stop himself, he wanted to give her time to say no.

She didn't, standing up, rising to her toes and brushing incredibly soft lips over his in the lightest of butterfly touches. One of them moaned—him? Her? Then their mouths were fused together, a kiss that might have looked chaste to a passerby but that made the entire inside of his body turn to molten fire.

This—this wasn't just a kiss. This was everything he'd never known he wanted.

*   *   *

BEFORE NATE'S ARRIVAL, ALEXA had been stuck thinking about the passage from the book. She'd spent a long, sleepless night, questions racing through her mind—who had written it? Why was the book in Estelle's shop?

She wanted to believe that it wasn't real, and to forget that she'd ever found it. Nate's kiss—it did just that.

She hadn't been kissed at all in a long time, and never, ever like this.

When finally he pulled back, she couldn't stop from pressing her fingers to her lips with wonder. She'd never been the type to blush and stammer over a man—she'd grown up with far too strong of a role model.

But this simple touch from a man who was the next thing to a stranger—at a time in which neither of them, she was certain, were looking for anything like this?

It was very nearly her undoing.

"That... that was interesting." Running her tongue over her lips, she tasted him, watched his grey eyes darken, like an incoming storm.

He nodded, his muscles tensing, and for a brief, wild moment, she thought he might kiss her again.

Then he was gone and Alexa felt better, brighter, than she had since before her accident.

CHAPTER SEVEN

WHAT HAD POSSESSED HIM?

Nate had never been the kind of man who avoided intimacy, though some of his ex's might have argued that point. But the fact remained that he'd come to Florence for peace, and in his experience, that fairer sex were rarely peaceful.

But Alexa... Alexa was different. She was the furthest thing possible from a badge bunny, a woman who was just attracted to the uniform—and sometimes handcuffs—of a cop.

She ran deep. Though he was certain that those deep waters were not still, he was already in over his head and didn't want to be saved.

He ran the back of his hand over his mouth, trying to recall the way it had felt to have her soft lips pressed there.

The clanging of a locker door in the men's staff room tore the image away, reminding him to get his game face on. Daydreaming while on shift at a maximum security prison was suicide.

"Fury." The outgoing officer who held Nate's position, but on the night shift, nodded at him as Nate entered the cell block. Dylan Stark was a man about Nate's age, and he too carried shadows in his eyes.

Nate never asked, and Stark never offered. Still, the man was the closest thing to a friend that Nate had here in Florence.

"Anything I should know?" It was routine, to compare notes with the outgoing officer before the shift changed over. Knowing which inmates were sick, or feuding with one another, even those who had recently lost or gained privileges could mean the difference between life and death.

A few days ago, avoiding that fate had been mechanical, something that Nate knew he ought to do, but hadn't cared much about either way. In fact, the cop shrink back in LA would probably have argued that he was tempting fate because he felt like he didn't deserve to be alive.

Now, with Alexa's taste still on his lips, Nate felt the promise he'd made to her tugging at the corners of his mind, sparking to life things that had lain dormant for months.

The measured look that Stark leveled at him told Nate that the other man had noticed the change in him, but their relationship wasn't one that allowed for personal comments. So he waited, silent, for Stark to fill him in.

"Pretty quiet night." Stark nodded down the line of cells. Once Nate was on shift, the doors would unlock, and the inmates would be escorted to breakfast.

Nate nodded, was about to head off to meet up with the other guards who would help him escort the cell block to the dining hall, when Stark spoke again.

"Keep an eye on Higgins, though." Stark's face was, like Nate's, set in impassive lines—but something in his eyes made Nate stop to listen.

"What's going on?" That hint of curiosity that had led him

into the police force tried to sprout, but Nate tore it out by the roots. He was here to keep order, and nothing else.

"Nothing concrete." Now Stark turned and looked Nate square in the face, and Nate knew what he would say before he did. "Just a sixth sense, I guess. He's dangerous. I just don't know why."

Nate nodded in thanks before Stark strode off, and though no one would have known it to look at him, he kept his fellow guard's words in mind as he and the other guards started to open the cells, organizing the inmates for the march to breakfast.

In a place like this, where every single inmate had done something pretty fucking bad to land them there in the first place... for Stark to comment on this one particular man?

Nate would pay attention.

There was too much to do, to pay attention to, to single the man out before the men were all seated with their trays, eating bowls of grey sludge that masqueraded as oatmeal. But as Nate patrolled the tables, he found Higgins sitting at the far end of a mostly empty one, hunched over his bowl, eating steadily.

He'd had a vague recollection of the man's face when Stark had mentioned his name. But now he studied the man with a vague sense of foreboding.

The Native American was young, in his mid-twenties, if Nate remembered correctly. There was nothing overly sinister from his appearance, nothing to set him apart from the other men—his dark hair, though long, was tied back neatly in a knot with a scrap of cloth, probably torn from a sheet, and though his moustache was unfashionable, it was neatly groomed. Nate had never liked the dark webbing of tattoos that inked the skin of his temples or cheeks—thin lines with slender but menacing spikes—but again, more inmates had ink than not.

But there was something about this young man that was vaguely... off. That notion was only reinforced when Higgins looked up to find Nate watching him, and Nate saw the strange flicker in his night dark eyes.

Like a lightning flash in a pitch dark sky, it hurt his eyes before vanishing entirely. Then the sullen man returned to his meal, shoveling it in with a ferocity that said he didn't find the taste nearly as revolting as Nate found the appearance.

The man ate steadily, moving from his oatmeal to apple without appearing to have any interest in or even knowledge of the other men surrounding him. Nate was so intent on figuring out what, exactly, made the seemingly inoffensive inmate seem so strange that it took a second before the whispered comment penetrated his consciousness.

"Now!"

Nate turned just in time to see the prisoner who'd been seated back to back with Higgins—Rorman, Nate thought his name was—turn, so quickly that if Nate hadn't been looking he would have missed it.

"Motherfucking rapist!" The other man's bald head gleamed as he dropped a small milk carton onto Higgins' head, before letting out a triumphant shout, shooting a look around that dared anyone to come close.

Nate was already moving when the contents of the carton—a biological cocktail that it was best not to ruminate on the contents of—started to cascade down Higgins' head.

His eyes met Nate's as he rose, and the blank insanity in their depths chilled his blood.

With a howl, Higgins launched himself at Rorman, and Nate caught a glimpse of something metallic in the man's hand. The scene before him slowed, and he heard his own breath roaring in his ears as he grabbed for his baton and plunged himself into the fray.

"Break it up! Now!" He knew the words would fall on deaf ears... by now every inmate in the entire hall had closed in, circling the small group, anticipating the fight. The noise was deafening, but Nate was focused entirely on the two men at the center.

He'd been certain that he'd seen the flash of something in Higgins' hand, and was sure that the man had had a shiv. But now, in close, it was Rorman whose fist was closed around a weapon, a crude sliver of plastic that had been filed to lethal sharpness.

Higgins had the rage of the insane on his side, but Rorman was nearly twice the younger's man size—and Nate was pretty sure that if Higgins had a weapon, Rorman had help in disarming him.

Maybe he shouldn't have cared whether the men here lived or died. But even without a badge on his shirt, the feeling was the same—he was here to protect.

He'd been in dangerous situations before, but it never got easier—the sickly surge of adrenaline, the knowledge that every decision you made had to be the right one.

The one with the weapon was his primary concern. Lunging like he was back in high school football, he wrapped his arms around Rorman's waist and tackled him to the ground.

The man howled, and heat spread in a thin line over Nate's shoulder.

He'd been stabbed. Twisting, he tried to get his hand on the weapon, and was rewarded with a fist in the eye, another in the jaw. Higgins was behind him, spittle flying as he tried to get at his attacker; Nate kicked out with both feet to get him the hell out of the way.

His muscles strained as he wrestled Rorman down and over, then shoved his face into the floor. As he cuffed him another officer rushed in to help restrain him, and Nate heard the alarms—one of his fellow officers had pressed the panic alarm and other guards were on their way.

Two officers took charge of Rorman.

"You're going to solitary," one said as Rorman was dragged toward the door. The prisoner just grinned.

"Rapists don't deserve to share space with the rest of us." The rest of the prisoners in the hall let out a cheer even as they were herded into lines to be escorted back to their cells.

Strange bit of prison culture, that, Nate thought as he grimaced and pulled himself to his feet. He tried not to pay too much attention to who had done what to land them behind bars, but Rorman had been convicted of killing three men. Yet he and the other inmates considered him, and most others, a better man than one who had harmed a woman or a child.

Case in point—no one had come to the aid of Eugene Higgins, a fact, Nate saw, that had not been lost on the prisoner. As Higgins was escorted toward the door himself, a safe distance behind Rorman, he looked back over his shoulder at Nate.

"We pals now. Right, man?" "Shut it," barked the officer in charge of him, but Higgins looked to Nate.

Having decent relationships with the inmates was important for maintaining order. But at the same time, they had to be reminded of who was in control.

Nate opened his mouth to reply in the negative, but Higgins was gone. Only then, when a medic came at him, did Nate realize that a hot, sticky trail of blood was dripping down his arm—and that the place where he'd felt that heat during the fight was throbbing with white hot pain.

He'd been stabbed with a goddamn shiv, and in that moment, rather than thinking that he'd deserved it...he was fucking pissed.

*   *   *

ALEXA POSITIONED A RICKETY kitchen chair under the ceiling trapdoor that led to the attic and climbed up onto the cracked vinyl seat. She lectured herself as she stretched up to brace her hands inside the hole, thinking that this really was a good hiding place for things, because it was so frigging hard to get up here.

A whisper of thought told her that maybe it was a sign—that she should leave well enough alone. But she hadn't been able to get the book out of her mind all day. The more she thought about the book, the more she felt like she was on the cusp of catching hold of her own memories of the accident.

Bracing her hands, she prepared to swing herself up into the darkening attic. She'd grab the book and hurry down—a thunderstorm had started up outside, dimming the late afternoon light, and she knew that the attic would not be a most welcoming place.

The shrill chime of a bell made her jolt and shriek, and the chair slipped, sending her crashing to the floor. Her heart pounded wildly, adrenaline making her see stars, as she gained her bearings and realized that the unfamiliar sound was that of a doorbell.

She hadn't come across one at any other entrance, so she assumed that the ringing was coming from downstairs, outside the shop. Picking herself up off the floor and wincing at the ensuing stiffness in her limbs, she limped down the stairs, through the cooler, and to the front door of the flower shop.

"Come in, come in." Undoing the deadbolt, she ushered him inside, then shut the door against the storm outside. He wasn't wearing a jacket and was soaked to the skin. "What the hell are you doing out there without a coat?"

He didn't answer with words, instead holding up a white plastic bag from which wafted the scent of Chinese takeout. As she set the food aside on the counter, she discovered that it wasn't what had her mouth watering.

She hadn't seen Nate without his uniform before, and now he stood before her in faded blue jeans and a white T-shirt that was plastered to his skin with rain. She did her best not to ogle, but the thin fabric made it very clear that what she'd suspected was a nicely formed body was even better than she could have imagined.

Her attention wandered over that nicely formed torso, and she felt her body tighten in response. When she noted the hint of pink bleeding through one shoulder of the shirt, she moved to press her hand to it without thinking.

"What happened?" Her fingers tugged at the fabric of his sleeve, peeling it back to discover a bandage, once white, now stained from the hint of blood that the rain had teased out. "Nate. You're hurt."

His hand caught hers around the wrist and she pulled back from the wound sharply, afraid she'd hurt him. But when she looked up into his face, she found that it wasn't pain on his face.

It was grief. It was desire. It was so many things that she too felt, too many for one person to face alone.

"I need you." This was all he said, and then those strong arms of his had clasped her around the waist, lifted her until her bottom was settled on the counter. One of his hands splayed flat over her back, pressing her closer and closer until there was nothing between but the heat they created. The other hand tangled in her hair, and Alexa swore that she could feel the air around them crackle with whatever it was that hung between them.

His lips came down on hers with an intensity that spoke of a need that went far beyond the physical. They were strangers still, and yet each soul recognized, yearned for, needed the other.

It was in no way rational, and yet it still was.

Nate's mouth slanted over hers, hungry and hot and not a little bit desperate. Alexa felt her head tip back under the onslaught, and he took advantage of the exposed column of her throat, kissing his way down to her collarbone and yanking her hips forward until her core cradled his hardness.

She didn't know him well enough to know his mannerisms, his habits, but in that moment she was certain that he needed some kind of solace that, inexplicably, she was the only one able to provide.

She'd be a cruel woman to turn him away. A stupid one as well, because when she was pressed against him like this, she felt safe in a way that she hadn't since the moment she woke up in that hospital bed, a chunk of her memory gone.

Alexa waited for his hands to move to the expected places, eager for the touch, which anchored her in the now and kept her from worrying about the past or the future. But even as her legs clamped around his hips and she moaned in surrender, he pressed a finger to the pulse beneath her jaw and then placed one final kiss on her forehead before drawing back.

"I'm sorry. I need to eat something." He grimaced, gesturing to the wound on his shoulder. "I'd like to play the big tough guy for you, but if I'm honest, I'd tell you that I probably need to sit down too."

"Can you make it up the stairs?" Alexa was instantly concerned, and even tried to pull back as Nate clasped her around the waist and helped her off the counter. He cast her that mysterious little half smile that made her insides do funny things, and laced his fingers through her own.

"Physically, it's just a cut. It's not that deep. Didn't even need stitches." His face was cast in shadows from light made dim by the thunderstorm outside. "I just... I have a thing about blood. It's been a long day."

Alexa's gaze raked over his face—it was on the tip of her tongue to make a teasing comment about such a big guy being afraid of a bit of blood. But there was something in his tone that stopped her, had her tightening her fingers in his own and pulling him towards, then through the cooler, and up the stairs into the apartment.

"I can throw your clothes in the dryer, if you'd like." Alexa offered this shyly. It must have been hellishly uncomfortable having the wet clothing pulling at his skin, but it might be even more uncomfortable for them both if he took her up on her offer, because she had nothing for him to wear in the meantime.

He studied her face for a long moment, and Alexa felt her heart thud with anticipation when he finally nodded.

"I'd appreciate that. If you have a blanket or something, I'll wrap that around myself." Eyes on her, he reached for the hem of his sodden T-shirt, pulling it up and over her head in one breathtaking move, and Alexa swallowed hard at the sudden view of dusky skin pulled tight over planes of muscle. He was thinner than he should have been, given his height and frame, and she wondered if the reason he'd lost weight was the same reason that he carried that haunted look in his eyes.

As she stared, his hands moved to the waistband of the jeans. The sudden charge in the air arcing between them told her in no uncertain terms that, feeling well or not, if she stayed put, this was going to move to the next level *now*.

While part of her wanted that more than she'd wanted anything in her life, Alexa found herself spinning on her heel and retreating to the bedroom to get the duvet.

Her life was in a state of flux. While she was incredibly drawn to him, there was still a tiny corner of her brain—the area that housed common sense—that told her to slow down.

Alexa kept her eyes fastened to the floor as she held the quilt out to Nate. Still, her imagination didn't seem to need a visual—it was flooding her mind's eye regardless.

Face flushed, she hurried to the kitchen and busied herself opening the containers of take-out that he'd brought over, dawdling over it until she was certain that he'd be well covered. Only then did she carry over the cardboard boxes of cashew chicken and of something else with vegetables and noodles that she couldn't quite identify, holding both out to him to choose.

He took the unidentifiable one.

"What is that?" Alexa asked, sitting down next to him on the couch. His body shifted so that he was facing her, and the tight wrap of the quilt opened up as he did, revealing a slice of hard male torso.

Alexa kept her gaze firmly fixed on his face, even as her hormones went wild.

"Tofu." Nate scooped up a large bite, groaning as the taste hit his tongue. The sexual sound made Alexa warm—very, very warm. "I've been a vegetarian for several years."

Pinning Alexa with a wry smile, he winked before taking another bite. The food was definitely doing him good—more color was appearing in his cheeks. Alexa knew hers were flushed too, but it had nothing to do with bringing her blood sugar up.

"This is the part where I say something hugely original like, where do you get your protein, right?" Alexa took a bite of her own dinner, though just being around Nate had her so excited that she didn't have much of an appetite. Still, he'd taken the trouble to come here to see her, and had been thoughtful enough to bring a meal, so she'd damn well eat it.

Nate barked out a laugh. "Yes, that's usually the reaction." He studied her intently with those storm grey eyes. "Aren't you going to ask me why, or make some joke about getting some meat in me?"

Alexa raised an eyebrow before eating another bite of chicken and cashews. "I figure if you want me to know, you'll tell me."

Shutters lowered over Nate's eyes and Alexa sank her teeth into her tongue until she tasted the tang of blood. What had she said? She'd been trying to be sensitive.

For several minutes they ate in silence that had thickened with tension, Alexa dying to look up, to examine this fascinating creature in front of her. Then he cleared his throat, and when her eyes met his, she understood that what he was about to say carried heavy weight.

"I used to be a cop," Nate started, setting his empty container aside. "Worked in animal control for a while. Some of the things I saw… I started to have a hard time eating anything that had once been alive."

"Wow." He cocked his head to one side at the softly spoken word, and she continued. "That just makes my heart hurt. I don't think I could do a job like that. But that just makes me appreciate the people who do it all the more."

"Takes all kinds." Nate shifted on the couch, and Alexa's attention was again drawn to the hard muscle of his chest. Tearing her attention away, she forced herself to focus on what he was saying. "I could never do what you do, for example."

"The flowers or the art?" Alexa raked a hand through her hair with frustration. She was still trying to find her way around the shop, and she hated the sense of disorientation. "Because I won't be able to do the flowers for very long."

"Isn't it a kind of art?" Nate took Alexa's now empty container for her, and the slight brush of fingers made her pulse race. "It seems like it, at least when you do it."

The compliment made her tingle. "That part, I could do. It's the rest—the dealing with people."

She smirked. "Too much time spent dealing with the public makes me twitchy. I don't actually like people very much."

"I don't know if I believe that," Nate grinned, settling back on the couch. This was the most at ease that Alexa had seen him so far. "You were pretty friendly to me when I came in."

"I said I don't like people, plural," she replied primly, though in truth the back and forth banter, the flirtation, had her feeling like she'd drunk just a sip too much champagne—effervescent and giddy. "Certain individual people are exempt, of course."

Nate placed his hand on her foot, the movement again opening up the blanket, and when he pinned her with his stare Alexa felt her pulse begin to skitter. "Do I count as an individual, then?"

"Of course." Unable to hold the intensity of his look, she found herself looking down at her own intertwined fingertips. "So if you were a cop, why do you work at a prison now?"

That same look of censure passed over his face, and Alexa could have kicked herself. Lord, but she was just useless at flirting. Hell, he hadn't even told her where he worked, she'd just taken note of his uniform—was it creepy to pay that much attention? She had no idea.

But instead of condemning her as nosy, he held her stare, then slowly spoke, turning the question back on her. "Why are *you* here?"

"I'm here to remember." She spoke on instinct, without taking the time to think about it—but now she wondered which memories, exactly, had become more important to her.

Against the blanket Nate's hand flexed, tightening before letting go.

"I'd rather forget."

*   *   *

THE BUZZ OF THE DRYER cycle finishing broke through the intense moment. Alexa bounced off the couch with relief evident in every muscle of her body.

Nate watched with narrowed eyes as she scurried down the hall to get his clothes. What was her deal? His cop instincts told him that there was more to her than met the eye, but was she deliberately hiding something?

His gut said no.

Why did he even care? He shouldn't—in fact, he should walk away right now before getting in any deeper. He couldn't believe that he'd told her that he'd been a cop, had been on the verge of telling her about his partner—he'd tried so hard to leave the past in the past, and out of Florence.

The fading light cast intriguing shadows on her curvy figure as she made her way back toward him, hands smoothing out wrinkles in his now dry clothes. When their gazes caught, he felt a funny little squeeze in his heart.

He'd never been one to believe in those instant connections that people talked about. If it wasn't real, wasn't something he could reach out and touch, he tended to be skeptical.

But Alexa? He'd wanted her from the first moment he'd seen her, in the diner, sketching away furiously on a napkin. It wasn't just lust, though he had a healthy dose of that too.

There was something in her, some spark of life that drew the darkness inside of him.

He wanted her, and he wasn't a good enough person to let her go.

She busied herself in the kitchen while he dressed again. He was amused and intrigued by the fact that she was so embarrassed at having him dress around her. If they headed where he wanted to go, she'd be getting over that mighty quick. But he found it sweet—the flush of pink that tinged her cheeks as she walked him down the stairs and to the door of the flower shop made him feel alive.

Leaving her, knowing he was going home to the dark, was not a happy thought.

"Why are you so sad?"

Nate whipped his head around—she'd caught him by surprise. That he was often miserable wasn't something he hid from people, but most people didn't comment on it. Didn't want to risk being pulled into something that took them out of their own self-absorbed worlds.

That she'd commented… it floored him.

Gently, he cupped her cheek in his hand, ran his fingers through the silky length of her hair, the scent of her shampoo wafting up to tease his nostrils—citrus and sugar.

He felt her pulse jump beneath his fingertips, heard her little intake of breath. Dipping his head, he pressed his lips to her ear.

"When I'm around you, I'm not sad." He trailed his lips across her cheek, until they just grazed her own. Felt her tremor answered inside his own chest. "May I?"

"Please." Her voice was shaky, a plea that he felt too.

The fingers that were threaded through her hair clenched; she gasped. His other hand came to rest on the sweet curve of her waist.

"Last chance." His voice was hoarse, and he felt the last dregs of his control slipping away as he pinned her with his stare. It was a warning for them both.

No matter how insane it was to feel this connection, it was there nevertheless. They were at the point of no return—one more kiss, and that indescribable thing between them would become a link that couldn't be broken.

Nate's mind screamed at him, reminding him that the noble thing to do would be to walk away. To keep her light far away from his dark.

He wasn't that strong. He didn't know if he'd get very far, anyway, not with the determined spark in the eyes of the woman in his arms.

"Kiss me." Two simple words, and yet they sliced like a knife, severing the remainder of his control.

He crushed her to him, savored the sensation of her softness against the hard planes of his own body. He swallowed her gasp, muttered a curse, and stroked his tongue over her lips, desperate for her to part them, to let him take them as deep as he could, as fast as possible.

Beneath him she moaned, and an answering sound rose from his throat. His lips moved like quicksilver, stroking over the incredible softness of her skin.

But even though she quivered against him, she was far from pliant in his arms. No, she was demanding, her hands roaming restlessly, her mouth taking what it wanted. The steel beneath the silk drove him crazy, in the best possible way, and he found himself, unbelievably, absolutely present in the moment. His entire being consumed with Alexa, and nothing else.

"Oh." The soft sound from her lips had heat flaring in his belly. Muscles taut with need, he stroked up with one hand, feathered it over the top of her breast, savored the sensation of her nipple pebbling beneath his palm.

His touch moved up, light but sure. The tips of his fingers dipped beneath the hem of her T-shirt, finding the hard ridges of scar tissue.

The idea that something had hurt her made him see red. He dipped his head, intending to run his lips over the wound, to soothe the hurt.

As his fingers played over the odd raised pattern, Alexa stiffened in his arms. Stiffened wasn't even the right word—her entire body went rigid, the warm, pliant flesh freezing into unyielding rigidity before he could even take a breath.

"What is it?" The words were barely out of his mouth when her hands were planted on his chest, shoving. And for such a small woman, she had strength. "Alexa. What's wrong?"

"Off. Off!" Her voice was a full-on scream as she flinched away, cowering against the counter. In front of his disbelieving eyes, she dropped to the floor, curled into a small ball—defending herself against an unknown enemy.

"Alexa." His heart thudded against his ribcage as he slowly, deliberately stepped back. Shoving away the demands of his body, he crouched down beside her, careful to not even brush against her. "Alexa, it's just me. It's Nate. There's no one else here."

It broke his heart to watch her quiver. But as though exerting the strength of her mind over her body, she relaxed muscle after muscle, unfurling from the tight defensive position.

Her eyes, when she finally sat up and looked at Nate, were full of mortification.

"I am so sorry." Alexa hugged her arms to her chest, her face flushing crimson. "I don't know what the hell happened. You touched my scars, and it… I had déjà vu."

"Anything you want to share?" Nate kept his voice deliberately casual. He of all people understood wanting to keep one's demons hidden.

Raking trembling fingers through her hair, Alexa blinked up at him, then worked her way back to standing. "I was… in a bad car accident. I can't tell you more than that, because I don't remember. But that's where I got the scars. I… when you touched them it must have triggered something."

"Did it make you remember anything?"

Alexa hesitated, then shook her head. "No. It's like… the memories are right there, so close I can almost see them, touch them, taste them. But I just can't grab hold of them, no matter what I do."

Her tone was colored with frustration, and the way that she avoided him eyes told him that there was something more, something she wasn't telling him.

The cop in him wanted to push.

Despite these strange feelings between them, though, he had no right.

"You can tell me, you know." Though his arms ached to hold her, to soothe away the wild look in her eyes.

If he did, she'd bolt, and possibly never come back again.

This time when she looked up at him, weariness was etched in every line of her face, putting his heart in a virtual fist and squeezing tight.

"I can't tell you what I don't remember." Her words were heavy, and Nate suddenly understood that, no matter what his own issues were—they paled in the face of whatever this woman was carrying inside of her.

He wanted to press. But he understood enough to refrain.

"I should go." The way her arms wrapped around her body, the hunch of her shoulders, all told him that she desperately wanted to be alone.

"Thank you." Alexa whispered, her words raw.

He'd honor what she wanted. He'd be an ass not to. But he wasn't going to let her pull away.

He knew firsthand the trouble that came with that route.

"Alexa." He waited until she looked up, then made a show of fisting his hands at his sides. Slowly, giving her plenty of time to stop him, he leaned in.

She didn't stop him, so he brushed the most gentle of kisses over her lips.

The confusion in her eyes nearly broke his heart.

"I'll see you soon." Though it went against everything in him to walk away from a woman in need, he was not about to presume that he knew better than she did.

So with that light kiss burning his lips, he forced himself to walk away, waited until he heard the click of the door locking behind him.

As he walked home, he wondered what secrets lay in the memory of Alexa Kendrick.

CHAPTER EIGHT

ALEXA RETRIEVED THE BOOK before she could talk herself out of it. Needing to feel sheltered, she retreated to the small bedroom where she had been sleeping, creating a nest out of sheets and the comforter that held the scent of Nate's skin.

What the hell had just happened?

Nate had been kissing her. More than that, *she* had been kissing *him*. For the first time in what felt like forever, she'd felt complete, as though the missing chunk of her memory had never existed in the first place.

Then Nate had brushed his fingers over her scars. Just a light touch, nothing that made her feel threatened. Out of nowhere images had exploded behind her eyes, so bright and so fast that she hadn't been able to catch on to any of the strings long enough to follow them back to their source.

She'd definitely seen barbed wire, inky and black, like that which had taunted her outside of the prison. There had been an impression of the attic, the one right above her head, as well as the damn mysterious book that was currently sitting in her lap.

There had also been her father. She barely remembered the man, and her mother certainly hadn't kept any photos of him around. In fact, she wasn't entirely sure that she'd recognize him if he walked right up to her on the street. Yet, there he had been, more an impression of him than a concrete image, along with a whisper of the word *sorry*.

That was it. Not much, but when combined all together with a dizzying fear of needing to escape or else lose her life, enough to send her into blind panic.

She was mortified that she'd reacted like that in front of Nate—worse, while he'd been touching her, because she wanted to do a hell of a lot more touching. But it had been a knee jerk reaction, that blinding fear, the scarlet pain.

Was it... could it have been part of a memory? Something from the accident?

But what did her accident have to do with her father, or this book?

"Just open it," Alexa muttered to herself as she stared down at the book. It was such a nondescript object, just a pain black book, but the one glimpse she'd already had of the inside made her stomach roil.

Her fingers were cold as she slowly, carefully, drew back the cover, then skimmed over the entry that she'd already read.

The words made her faintly sick, as they had the first time. But now she pushed herself to carry on.

I picked her out of all the girls there that night. You could tell from lookin' that the rest was all skanks. Whores. Dirty girls. But this one, she was clean. She was bright. Light. And I was dark.

Alexa was overwhelmed with the urge to slam the book closed, to take it back up to the attic or, even better, to burn it and flush the ashes down the sink. But something urged her on, and though she couldn't quite believe what the words were telling her, she kept on reading.

Girls like that, they're easy to fool. Trust just oozes out of them, like sweat, ya know? They want to think that everybody's good. Or that they can fix the bad ones, make them come around.

But when I picked her out, when I started to watch her, I already knew. I knew what I was going to do to her.

I was going to get her to trust me, to think of me as a nice guy. I was going to get her alone. Then I was going to rob her, beat her, take her.

Maybe I'd even kill her. Just 'cause I could.

Nausea swept over Alexa, one huge wave. Retching, she rose to her knees, not sure if she needed to run to the bathroom or not.

The urge to empty the contents of her stomach subsided, but the chill, the cold sweat, did not.

"Who are you?" Alexa ran her fingers over the book, which she'd slammed closed, her heart thudding against her ribcage.

She had… she had too many thoughts swirling through her head.

What *was* this book? It read like a journal… but whose? Why were they just photocopies, and not the real pages?

The handwriting looked male, and the narrator was speaking about what they would do to a woman.

Who had this happened to? The fact that it was hidden so carefully in the attic made her think…

It couldn't have been Estelle, her… her grandmother. Ellie would have found it while she was sorting through the attic.

Did that mean... had it happened to Ellie?

Why did she have the overwhelming sensation that her father was somehow involved, too?

Her mind reeled, and she felt the panic that she'd managed to evade after the accident, slamming into her with full force. It left her shaking, clammy, short of breath, unable to keep still—rising from the bed, she began to pace the confines of the tiny bedroom.

Maybe... maybe she was focusing too much on what she *didn't* remember. Maybe... maybe she needed to try to zero in on what *was* still in her fragile memory.

Breathing deeply, Alexa sank back down to the bed, wrapping herself in the comforter. The faint hint of Nate's scent that clung to it shouldn't have comforted her so much, and yet it reminded her of his promise—that she'd be safe when he was there.

Her mother had drummed it into her from childhood, not to let herself rely on any man. But needing to lean on someone and wanting to share the burden were, as she was rapidly coming to understand, not the same thing at all.

"Focus, Alexa. What do you remember?" She squinted as her mind whirled. This was harder than she'd anticipated.

Thinking back to the days after the accident, after she'd been patched up and started to heal... she remembered confessing her frustration to one of the doctors, a younger woman.

"Why can't I remember anything?" She'd felt so impotent, so *useless.* All she knew was what had been told to her—that she'd been in a tragic car accident, and that she was the only survivor. There was no one else involved with whom to share her burden.

The doctor had smiled gently, but Alexa had seen the shadows, even what she thought might be rage in the other woman's eyes. But when the doctor clasped Alexa's hand in her own and replied, her voice was calm and soothing.

"Sometimes events are so traumatic that our awareness rejects them." The doctor had spoken slowly, clearly trying to find the right words. "The brain… tucks them away, until we're able to handle them."

"Will I ever remember?" Alexa remembered almost screaming with frustration, the doctor's hand squeezing her own.

"You might. You might not." That rage again, so carefully contained. "But if you don't… it just might be for the best."

At the time Alexa had been too tired to argue that. But now… now she knew that it was time. Time to push through the shadows and find the truth, even if that truth was something she ultimately wished she'd left alone.

So what *did* she remember?

She had gone for a drink. Why? She was… she was celebrating a sale. Yes. Jia had called her that afternoon to tell her about one of her pieces selling for an astronomical amount of money.

She'd been flying high, sitting there alone, and savoring her drink. She'd felt as though she'd finally proven, mostly to herself, that she could stand on her own two feet—that she didn't intend to live in the shadow of her mother's money.

"I went for a drink, then… what?" Alexa recalled the image of sitting in the bar. She'd been sitting on a bar stool, swinging her feet with joy. She could almost taste the vinegar of the cheap wine she'd drunk.

But when she tried to push past that image, her memory threw up a barrier. A great concrete wall, and when she rammed her fist against it, terror swooped down to clasp her in its greedy fingers. Sitting on the bed, clammy sweat slicked her skin as she rapidly retreated from the fear.

Maybe… maybe she really didn't *want* to remember. Maybe she wasn't ready.

"But I know what happened, damn it." She'd been told— she'd been in a car accident. While she had to work through her survivor's guilt, she understood and accepted that. She'd almost died. She'd spent nearly a month in the hospital, two weeks of it in a coma.

So if she knew and accepted that, intellectually speaking… why couldn't she call up the actual memories?

"Argh!" Frustrated beyond words, Alexa stood, venturing out beyond the confines of the bedroom. Creamy yellow light from the street lights outside striped the shadows of night, and were a direct parallel, it seemed, to her mind.

Some things well lit, and easy to see. . . and some shrouded in the dark.

Her restless feet carried her to an old armchair that was lumpy with age. Curling into it, she stared out the window, squinting at the lines of the prisons that she could see in the distance.

The other, more immediate question was… what did her father have to do with any of this? Her best guess was that the trauma of the car accident had shaken loose some memories of the only other big trauma in her life, the death of her father.

Her mother never spoke of it, and Alexa had always assumed that he had died while he was still with them. But these little snippets of memory…

Was it possible that they had parted ways before his death?

"What the hell does it matter, anyway? Why do I care?" Great. Now she was talking to herself. But while she was… well, she had a point.

Why *did* she care? Why was she even here? She'd come because she'd felt drawn to get to know the sister that she'd never known she had… but Ellie had taken off, leaving Alexa alone, mired in her own uncertainty.

Maybe it wasn't a matter of focusing on what she remembered rather than what she didn't… maybe she needed to stop fixating on the past and live in the present. She was young, she was thankful to be alive. She was on a journey to explore who she was, and she had an incredibly exciting connection with the sexiest, most complex man she'd ever met.

A sudden flash, a visual of Nate and those muscles she'd gotten a glimpse of that afternoon… of those lean thighs spread on either side of her body…

Alexa felt heat wash over her skin, burning away the anxiety. Reaching for it, she clasped it tightly with both hands.

Why was she focusing on the past when the present had the potential to be so damn good?

*   *   *

ALEXA STOOD BY THE tiny window in the apartment's bathroom as she brushed her teeth before bed. The woman next door, the one who had dropped the bomb about remembering Alexa before running away with her freebie flowers, was taking out her garbage, rattling the cans in a way, it seemed to Alexa, to make as much noise as possible.

Alexa watched blankly for a few minutes as the woman set the cans on the curb. She thought about offering to help the elderly lady, but the way that Mrs. Gunderson thumped the lids down on the metallic cans made Alexa worry that perhaps she would get thumped, too.

This lady remembered Alexa. Her memories held things that Alexa's did not.

Her body tensed, itching to go down and demand answers from the woman.

Remembering the stubborn set of the older woman's mouth, she didn't think she'd get very far. So after she spat and rinsed off her toothbrush, she did the next best thing.

She called her mom.

It might be best left alone, true enough. But... she had to know.

"Alexa!" Her mother didn't bother with a salutation, launching right into the conversation. "I've been worried."

Was it normal worry? Or was it because her mother was keeping things from her?

Was she imagining things?

"Sorry," she replied automatically, returning to the chair in the living room. It was old and lumpy, yes, but it also fit her just right when she curled up and tucked her legs beneath herself. "Everything's fine."

"Ready to come home yet?" On the other end of the line, her mother laughed lightly... was Alexa imagining the strain that she heard underneath the words?

"Not quite," Alexa replied quietly, and her mother's laugh faded into silence. "I... I came across a place that seemed familiar. A flower shop."

"Is that so?" No pause, but this time Alexa was certain that she wasn't imagining the tension.

"The lady next door to the shop remembers you." In for a penny.

"Hmm." Her mother didn't even reply with words, and Alexa cringed. She wasn't sure what she'd expected, maybe flat out denial. Anything but the admission with silence that Tracy had been keeping secrets.

"Are you okay, Mom?" Alexa phrased the question cautiously, but inside… she wasn't feeling gentle. No… she was angry.

"I'm fine." Tracy's voice was clipped, and Alexa's anger surged. *She* was mad? She wasn't the one finding out how many things in her life had been a lie.

"You sound funny," Alexa pushed. Given her mother's temperament, it wasn't the smartest thing to do, but she found she was past the point of caring. "Are you sure nothing's wrong?"

"I'll be fine as soon as you come home where you belong!" Tracy's voice snapped out, the crack of a whip felt through the phone, and Alexa did something she'd never done before.

She hung up on her mother.

The phone rang again immediately, and Alexa turned it off before tossing the thing across the room. Sinking into the chair, she stared across the dark room into nothing.

Her mother always made so much noise, it had become habit to tune most of it out, to dismiss things out of hand. But this…

Tracy seemed so very adamant that Alexa not go poking into things best left alone. And maybe that was a sign, the universe telling Alexa to smarten up and pay attention.

Maybe instead of poking around Florence for secrets, she should go back to Phoenix, to her life. To painting. Move out of her mother's, get an apartment.

She thought of the book, of Nate... and knew that she couldn't. She'd started down the path of something, and she didn't think there was any turning back now. If she did, she'd always wonder what she didn't know about herself, be it about her past or about what she could have had with Nate.

Though she hadn't known it when Ellie had first approached her at the Boxtree... Alexa was beginning to see that understanding her childhood might be the key to making peace with the now. Why, she didn't know, because no matter how she turned it over in her head, she couldn't find a connection.

Yet, there it was, and ruminating on it more just brought the familiar frustration.

Inhaling deeply, she made a conscious effort to focus on the now. What did she want, right now?

The realization made her smile.

CHAPTER NINE

THE WEIGHT OF SURVIVOR'S guilt was nowhere to be found on Nate the next morning as he entered the prison.

Ever since Jud had been shot, Nate had spent most of his time in a haze of numbness. It was easier that way—so much easier than being overwhelmed by all the emotions that were forever simmering just below the surface. But this morning, for the first time in memory, he hadn't woken desperate for a drink.

That knowledge called Alexa to mind. Her reaction last night had triggered several of the cop instincts that just wouldn't stay dormant.

With a clearer head, he was able to sort that through. It was clear that she'd suffered some kind of trauma, but he didn't understand her bafflement over it. Had she tucked it away so deep that she truly didn't remember?

Stranger things had happened.

But even with the fragility of her confusion, beneath it was a visible core of steel. The woman was mysterious and yet adorable, cute with her kitten T-shirts and yet sexy... she was just a breath of fresh air, one of the most interesting people he'd ever met.

Sexy, he thought as he slammed the metal door to his locker shut. Yeah, she was sexy. Sexy enough that he'd had a hard time being a gentleman last night, when he was wearing nothing but his boxers and the blanket that smelled of her, and she was trying so hard to pretend that she wasn't looking.

"Hey, Fury!" Foster, one of Nate's fellow correctional officers, banged through the door to the men's room with enough force to make Nate wince.

"Foster." Apart from Stark, Nate hadn't welcomed any sense of camaraderie with his coworkers. He was just here to do his job, to pass the time.

Foster was one of those who never took a hint.

Foster, a man in the vicinity of forty with a stocky build and thinning hair that he buzzed down to the scalp, bellied over to Nate with his phone outstretched. "Hey, Fury. Want to see a picture of my wife's tits?"

What the fuck?

"No, thanks. I'm good." Nate kept his face impassive as the other man leered at him.

Prison guards were a strange breed—he'd known this from the start. But clearly, some were stranger than most.

"Come on, take a look. If you like what you see, you can come on over some night." When Nate just stared, Foster laughed, clearly thinking that Nate was the strange one. "What? It gets the missus excited. Come on, take a look. She's got a huge rack."

"No." This time Nate shook his head as he tried to get around Foster. Jesus, what kind of a sick fuck just offered his wife up to another man in the locker room of a prison?

Foster glowered at him. "What's the problem? You getting your cookie sugared somewhere else?"

Nate shook his head and this time pushed right past the other man. But Foster's weird comments had played right into the thoughts he was having of Alexa, and he couldn't help but imagine what it would be like to sink into her body.

He should walk away. He'd known that, even before last night he'd known that, but the evidence of her trauma only strengthened the rationale. Yet, instead of dragging one another down, he thought that maybe, just maybe, they could take their broken parts and make a whole.

His brow furrowed with resolve as he strode into the guard's room where he had to check in before going out into the cell block.

For so many months now, he'd been content to just float along in a sea of nothingness. But once, once he'd been a man who'd gotten what he wanted.

Maybe that didn't have to change.

*   *   *

"NO, I'M SORRY, BUT I really don't feel qualified to do your wedding consultation. As I've said, I've taken down your information, and I'll have Ellie call you back as soon as she's back in town."

"I don't understand why you own a flower shop if you don't know what you're doing." The woman standing on the other side of Alexa's counter was young, maybe twenty, dressed in clothes that told Alexa that all of the girl's taste was in her mouth.

She was chewing gum with her mouth open as she glared suspiciously at Alexa, as though Alexa was making up the entire story, just to liven up her day.

"Again, I don't own the shop. I'm watching it for my sister until she gets back from a family emergency." Alexa was seconds away from screaming. This, *this* was why she didn't work with the public.

"Well, I really can't wait." The girl chomped on her gum and pointed her chin in the air.

"You just said that the wedding isn't until 2017." Alexa heard the temper in her own voice and did her best to tamp down on it—she might want to throttle Ellie for leaving her in this mess, but probably murdering a customer would be really bad for her sister's business. "I would say that that's plenty of time."

"And I would say that you need to stop being lazy do this freaking consultation now," the girl replied, smirking in a way that made Alexa's fingers twitch, "or I'll take my business elsewhere."

Alexa did her best not to pump a fist in the air, instead schooling her features into a polite smile. At least, that was the look she was going for—the way she was feeling, she made no guarantees. "That's your choice, of course."

"Why, I..." The girl, clearly not accustomed to being told no, looked as though she was about to stomp her feet and burst into a tantrum. Alexa held her breath, waiting for it. But instead the girl stormed out of the shop, the glass bells on the door jingling merrily over her head as she went.

"Sweet mother." Alexa buried her head in her arms on the counter, whimpering. "No more people. Please, no more people."

The shop's phone line rang. It was an urgent morning delivery. Then there was another. The third time it rang, Alexa found herself snapping as she answered it.

"Estelle's Blooms!" Her voice was so loud that she winced.

"That was... enthusiastic." It was Ellie, who sounded perplexed. "Why are you yelling? Is it raining? Sometimes it gets a little crackly when it storms, you just have to jiggle—"

"No, no. It's fine." Alexa spoke over her sister. It was in fact raining, but the line was fine. Everything was fine. No matter how much she resented having these responsibilities thrust on her, she still... well, she still wanted to prove that she could do them. Weird as that was.

"Oh. Okay." Ellie exhaled so loudly that Alexa winced. "How are things going? Did you figure everything out?"

"As much as I could." Alexa was surprised to find her voice a little frosty. But damn it, sisters or not—she was angry. She hadn't asked to have Ellie's responsibilities shoved into her lap. "I just turned down a wedding consultation."

She wasn't about to apologize, either. She was a painter, not a florist.

"Oh. Well, I kind of expected as much." For the first time since she'd met her, Ellie sounded awkward. "And look, I... I shouldn't have just dumped all of this on you. But everything with Gabe's dad happened so quickly, I was afraid that you'd just leave. And that I wouldn't be able to make you come back." The last words were said in a rush, as though Ellie had to spit them out or lose them, and despite her best efforts, Alexa found her heart softening.

"Well. It hasn't been all bad." And it really hadn't. She certainly hadn't found a new calling, but she was finding a rhythm, working at the shop during the day, feeling inspired to paint at night.

Seeing Nate.

Ignoring the book.

"The apartment is all right? Do you have everything you need?"

"It's been great, actually." Some things were a little bit outdated, but Alexa hadn't realized how much she'd missed living on her own. She loved her mother, but it was refreshing to come and go as she pleased, to not have to worry about someone worrying if she went out for dinner after work.

To account to herself, and no one else.

Ellie chattered on in her ear for a few minutes, talking about Florida and her in-laws, but Alexa's mind had circled back and landed on the book.

Was it Ellie, the woman in the entries?

The thought made her sick. It plagued her until her mouth opened of its own accord, interrupting Ellie mid-sentence.

"I looked in the attic," she blurted out, her voice again just a bit too loud. She knew that she didn't imagine the weighted pause from the other end of the line.

"Why?" From her talkative sister, this was a rather short answer. "There's nothing up there. Just old junk that I'm organizing."

Ellie's voice—it had shifted from friendly and conversational to flat and harsh. Alexa was more than a bit taken aback.

"I—" Alexa wasn't sure what to say, finally opting for the truth. "I... you said that the reason you found me was because of a box you found in the attic. So... I don't know. I guess I was just... looking."

"I've spent a lot of time cleaning it out." Again, Ellie's tone was not welcoming. "I'd really rather you just stayed out of there."

Her wishes were clear—the attic was off limits.

As Alexa hung up, she knew that she was too late. She'd found what Ellie had been hiding. But oh God, oh God, what did it mean?

That book... the journal, or whatever it was.

If she had to guess, based on the way it had been hidden and Ellie's response...

It had happened to Ellie. What the hell was she supposed to do with that information? Especially when her sister clearly didn't want her to know.

It plagued her throughout the day. When she finally closed up for the day, locking the door behind her with a decisive click, Alexa all but ran up the stairs, in a frenzy.

Starting in the living room, she opened drawers, plastic tubs, shook out books. Surely if Ellie was the woman in that book, there was a mention somewhere else. A newspaper clipping, *something*.

There was nothing mentioning a violent attack on a woman. In fact, there wasn't much of anything at all.

But in the bedroom that Alexa wasn't using, in the ornate table that stood beside the bed, she found something else.

Gingerly, Alexa lifted the enlarged photograph from the wood. Yellowed with age, it showed three people—a man, a woman and a child—and styles showed that it had clearly been taken in the eighties or nineties.

She recognized two of the people in it. In the back, with a tight perm twisting her strands of blonde hair, was Alexa's mother. And the imp in the front, in the denim ensemble—it was her.

Which meant that the utterly unfamiliar man must have been her father.

Feeling as though the air had been sucked from her lungs, Alexa gingerly turned the picture over.

Joseph, Tracy and Alexa. 1990.

What was left of her breath wheezed from her lungs. Lightheaded, Alexa sank down to her knees.

This—this was her father. She'd been under the impression that he'd died when she was two. Yet here they were, clearly a family unit, when Alexa was three.

How did Ellie fit into this?

Alexa's head could barely contain it all.

Before she could think it through, she found herself reaching for her cell, pulling up her mother's contact. They hadn't spoken since Alexa had hung up on her, and Alexa fully expected her mother's voice to be frosty when she answered.

Instead it was full of concern.

"Is everything all right?" An odd choice of words to lead with. She knew she wasn't imagining it—her mother was hiding things. Things that she had a right to know.

"Well, I don't know, Mom." Alexa heard the anger tightening her own voice. "I just found a family picture. You, me and Dad, when I was three. I thought he died when I was two."

There was a pause, and Alexa had just opened her mouth to continue when her mother spoke.

"This has nothing to do with you, Alexa." Tracy's voice was heavy like stone. "You need to leave this alone."

For the second time in her life, Alexa hung up on her mother. For a moment she just rocked back and forth where she was, kneeling on the carpet in the strange bedroom, in an apartment that had belonged to a grandmother she'd never known.

Finding out about her past? It wasn't bringing her the peace she'd hoped for. Suddenly she was on her feet, running—running out of the bedroom, out of the apartment, out of the entire damn building.

It was still raining, the wind wild—not quite a monsoon, but still a massive storm. Sheets of rain instantly soaked her to the skin, plastered her hair to her head, but she didn't feel the cold, fueled by a burn that she didn't quite understand, one that penetrated right to the marrow of her bones.

She ran until her lungs burned, and her sneakers sloshed, and the rain was coming down so hard that she couldn't see where she was going. She stopped for a moment to get her bearings, leaning back against a building as her chest heaved, her lungs desperate for breath.

She'd blindly run all the way to the other side of town. Much more, and she'd have been at the gates of one of the prisons.

The barbed wire was just barely visible in the grey. Alexa stared at it for a long moment before turning and starting her walk back.

No longer blindly fueled by emotion, the way home was miserable. Her clothes stuck to her, chafing her skin, and the icy rain made violent shivers wrack her body. The wild run had been over in the blink of an eye, but the walk back took forever and a day.

A dark figure lurked outside the flower shop as Alexa came into view, and she stiffened, stilled, fear prying fingers into her mind. Then the figure turned, looked her way, and she realized that it was Nate.

One step, two, and then she was running. In that moment she wanted one thing only—to be in his arms, and to let the fire of what was between them melt the jagged cold that had settled in her very core.

"*Alexa*. What the hell are you doing out in this weather?" Nate was shrugging out of his coat before he'd finished speaking, wrapping Alexa in the dry warmth. "Where are your keys? Damn it, what were you thinking?"

"No talking." Determined, Alexa freed her arms, used them to twine around him. "I need you, Nate. Now."

He opened his mouth to speak, but she cut him off, rising onto her toes and pressing her mouth to his. Feverish with need, she slid against him, urging him to relax into what they both wanted.

"Alexa. I can't do this when you're obviously upset." With a groan that gave away the effort, Nate tore himself away, steadied her with his arms. "It's not how it should be."

Trembling from something other than cold, Alexa looked up at Nate. He had a point, she knew he had a point, and yet right here, right now, she saw with more clarity than she ever had in her life.

"I know what I'm doing. I know what I want." Fisting her hands in the front of his shirt, she rose onto her toes, kissed him again, and this time the embrace was slow and sweet, drugging

108

her senses. "I can't explain it. We barely know each other. But right now, you're the only thing that's right in my world."

In response Nate crushed her to him, and his mouth moved over hers with a mastery than made liquid heat slide through her center. But her true undoing was what he said when he again pulled away.

"I can't explain it, either. But I know one thing."

She urged him to continue with the tilt of her chin. In response he slid his hands down, cupped her bottom, lifting her so that she could wrap her legs around his waist, so that they were pressed so tightly together that their heat generated steam.

"I know that when we're together... neither one of us is alone in the world. Not anymore."

Alexa felt her pulse accelerate at the words that so matched what she was feeling, but there was no time to dwell on it, not when Nate had lifted her bodily, carrying her into the shop, bracing her briefly to lock it—ever cautious. She buried her face in his neck when he reached the bottom of the stairs, the muscles of his arms moving against her as he mounted the stairs, her held tightly against him.

Slamming the door behind them, Nate pressed her back against it. The wood was cold against her back, a sharp contrast to the heat of Nate at her front, as he took her mouth in another drugging kiss.

"Are you absolutely sure?" When he asked again, Alexa groaned with frustration, then nipped at his neck.

"Damn it, Nate. Do you want me or not?"

"Oh, I want you." The wicked curve of those lips that never fully smiled should have warned her, but nothing, *nothing*, could have prepared her what came next.

His stare holding hers, Nate slid her down his body with excruciating slowness, giving Alexa the opportunity to feel every last, hard inch of his flesh. Her mouth went dry when she discovered just how much he wanted her.

"You play dirty," she murmured, her tongue sliding out to moisten lips that had suddenly gone dry.

He grinned, traced a finger over those lips, stepping back.

"I'm just getting started." His stare raked her over, lingering on her breasts, her center and making her temperature shoot up.

"Strip."

"I—what?" Surely he hadn't just... *ordered* her?

That little half smile that had come to be so familiar appeared, and Alexa felt her knees weaken. "You heard me. Unless you've changed your mind?"

"No," Alexa hastily fisted her hands in the hem of her sopping wet T-shirt. She wasn't sure what to think of his demand—surely this wasn't normal?

But being shocked had no effect whatsoever on whether or not she wanted to obey. Neither did the heat that flashed through his eyes when she peeled the wet cotton over her head and off.

His eyes gleamed, making no attempt to hide the way he was staring. But he didn't speak, didn't move and belatedly Alexa realized that he was waiting for her to carry out his order in its entirety.

To strip.

To be naked, as she had for no one before. She wasn't a virgin, but she wasn't very experienced either—and though it pained her to admit it, she'd never been entirely skin to skin with anyone in her life.

The realization made her falter, hands at the button of her jeans. But Nate was there, believing in her, and though it made no sense, not this soon, still she trusted him.

She worked her way from her jeans, kicked them aside. Reaching behind her, she tried to unfasten the clasp of her bra, and huffed with frustration when she couldn't.

"Let me." Then Nate's hands were on her, twining with hers, undoing the offensive garment. His fingers hooked in the sides of her panties, tearing them away, and shock rocked its way through her, understanding that this calm, patient man was anything but in this moment.

Alexa cried out when he parted her thighs, slid fingers through. Her knees buckled, and again he lifted her, balancing her weight in one arm while bringing his finger up between them with the other.

'This?" He said, rubbing his fingers together before sliding them down to cup her bottom. "This is mine."

"Oh, God." She'd never imagined this before—hadn't given much thought to sex in the last year at all. But with Nate taking charge, all she had left to do was to do, to *feel*.

She hadn't known, but it was what she needed. To be in control—she was pretty sure he needed that, too.

"Arms around me. Don't let go." Alexa had no intention of doing so, but still she tightened her grip as Nate carried her down the short hallway, and into the bedroom where she slept. His fingers kneaded her bottom, his arms holding her weight as he slowly, gently laid her down on the bed.

The room was dark, the only light from the street lamps outside. Alexa lay still, remaining how he had placed her. The way his eyes moved over her was so intense that her instinct was to reach for the blanket, to cover up—but what was in those eyes kept her still.

"Look at you." His voice was... reverent. Yes, that was the word. Reverent, as though he'd never seen anything as perfect as she was, right in that moment.

Alexa knew that she was anything but. She had scars from the accident, the spiked vine on her shoulders, her neck, more silvery lines on her torso, her thighs. Remembering, she twisted under his gaze, but when he approached the bed and slowly, gently placed the palm of his hand over her heart, Alexa forgot all about what she looked like, what he looked like—forgot everything but the emotion arching between them.

This—she'd never felt anything like this before. She wasn't sure that she ever would again.

"Lie still." The rough fabric of the denim pulling taut over his thighs created delicious friction over Alexa's skin as Nate straddled her, mid-thigh. Settling back on his heels, he began to stroke his hands over her, the touches designed to explore rather than arouse, but accomplishing the latter regardless.

One palm remained on her chest, counting the beats of her heart, while the other moved, tracing down between her breasts, under them, over her ribcage. Spanning her waist, smoothing the curve of her hips.

Grazing the place she most wanted him to touch before gently tracing the lines of her spread thighs. All the while being careful not to touch her scars.

"Nate." His fingers had brought fire to her veins, and she shifted restlessly beneath him, no longer able to keep still.

His eyes flashed when she said his name. Dipping his

head, he took her breast in his mouth, and the surge of sensation made Alexa cry out, her back arching.

She had so little experience that she'd thought she would be shy. But with Nate it was an exploration, almost a celebration, and because of that her nerves were gone.

"I love the way you respond." Pulling his mouth from her skin, Nate fixed his stare on her face, his other hand splaying over the curves of her breast to squeeze. His hands were hot, branding her skin.

"This shouldn't be all about me," Alexa finally managed to pant, her hands sliding down his taut shoulders, the hard planes of his back. She tugged at the cotton of his shirt until he barked out a laugh and pulled the offensive garment up and over his head.

"Ah, but when it's all about you? That's when it's about me, too." The corners of Nate's lips turned up a hint just before he dipped his head, pressed a kiss to her stomach, made the muscles there quiver.

He kissed his way down, swiped his tongue over her hipbone. Alexa reached for him, determined to do more than just *take*, but it was becoming quite clear that he was the one running this show. The weight pressing Alexa into the bed told her that, as he'd said, making it all about her was indeed arousing him.

She tensed for a moment when his mouth found the wet heat between her legs. She'd never done that before, never wanted to. But with Nate's hands holding her open, his murmurs working against her sensitive flesh, she could do nothing more than be carried away.

"Oh." Her hips arched against him; he caught them in strong hands, hauling her to the edge of the bed. "Oh!"

She was… she couldn't…

His mouth sent her shooting past a glittering line that she'd never crossed with another person, and she cried out, her hands reaching out blindly. As she crested, he held her tight, anchoring her as she let go.

She was dimly aware of being lain back on the bed gently, of the cold when he stood up. She heard the rasp of a zipper, the sound of his jeans falling to the floor. The crinkle of a wrapper that made her breath hitch with anticipation.

"Alexa." Nate urged her up further onto the bed, so that her head was cushioned by the pillows. He followed her, covering her with his body, and when his lean, naked length was pressed against her she couldn't hold back the shudder.

He kissed her then, long and deep, before circling her wrists with his hands. Raising them above her head, he curled her fingers around two of the wooden bars in the headboard.

"Don't move. I don't want you thinking about pleasing me. I just want you to take what I give you."

Oh, god.

Alexa had never imagined that words could be as arousing as touch, but everything he said just added to the storm brewing inside of her. Above her he drank in her responses, his breath rasping in and out every time that she quivered.

Only when her hands were securely clasped around the bars of the headboard did Nate press his hard length to her wet heat. He eased inside, and Alexa arched against him and cried out.

"You're so tight. Jesus. I can feel you, pulling me in." Slowly, his eyes trained on hers, he continued to enter her body. "Can you feel me?"

"God, yes." Alexa shuddered when he seated himself, her body shifting restlessly.

He wasn't wrong—she was tight. Her flesh wasn't sure whether to explode with desire or to ache, and when he started to move it was a combination of both.

Though she wanted to reach for him, to pull him close, the look in his eyes warned her to do as he said. So she clung tightly to the bars, her hands slick with sweat, as his slow, sure thrusts became harder, deeper. Choked cries escaped her lips, groans from his, but neither of them spoke beyond that, communicating only through their locked stares and the movements of their bodies.

He seemed to delight in her submission, and she found solace in the demands of his movement. As they moved, each of them fed the other until both were drunk off of the sensation.

Alexa felt that beautiful tension again rising inside of her, filling her to the point where she thought she might explode. His skin became slicked with sweat, his pace increasing, hips slapping together, and she knew he was nearing the end too.

She went over first, the world in front of her blurring as she found release. He followed immediately after, crushing her to him, burying his face in her hair as liquid heat warmed her from the inside out.

Their eyes met, and though Alexa opened her mouth to speak, there were no words. She felt strangely near tears when Nate gently eased her fingers from their tight grip, massaged the soreness away, and kissed her forehead. Pulling her to him, he rolled, and they ended up with her half splayed across his chest, the reassuringly steady beat of his heart beneath her cheek.

"I thought that I'd want you less, after having you." When Nate finally spoke, his voice was raw, as though he'd shattered into a million pieces and been put together again. "But I think it only made it worse."

"What is this?" Alexa asked, lifting her head to look at him. Her heart thudded against her ribcage when she saw her own myriad of emotion reflected there. "What I mean is... I don't have a lot of experience. But this... what's between us... It isn't usual. Am I right?"

Nate's hand played over her back, traced the wings of her shoulder blades in silence before he answered.

"I wanted you the second I saw you, sitting there in the diner, so absorbed in your art." Beneath her cheek, she felt his pulse skitter. "But I thought it was because we were alike in a way. Survivors."

Alexa wanted to stiffen at the reminder, but found that her limbs wouldn't cooperate.

Nate continued. "I've never been afraid of commitment. I'm not one of those guys. But I've also never felt anyone who made me want to stay."

His eyes met hers, and Alexa sucked in a breath.

"But now that I've had you in my arms, now that I've felt you tremble underneath me? I'm not sure that I'm ever going to be able to let you go."

CHAPTER TEN

NATE WOKE UP THE same way he had when he was a cop, pulled from a deep sleep to silent, watchful waking in a split second. His pulse throbbed as he propped himself up on his elbows, wondering what felt strange.

Alexa stood at the window, framed by sheer white curtains. Her back was to him, and as he watched the slight movements of her body as she breathed, felt himself relaxing as he remembered where he was, who he was with, he understood what was different—she was.

He didn't have any desire for a drink. He had woken up with his head above water, with no weight pressing down on his chest.

Knowing that it was because of her made his heart swell with feelings he never thought he'd feel. Feelings he still wasn't sure he deserved to have.

"Hey," he said softly, so many feelings pressing against his chest that he had to reach out to her or explode. "What are you doing?"

"I got up and I wanted to draw." Alexa turned just enough for him to see her profile. Her lips curved in a half smile as she held up her sketch pad for him to see.

It was a simple drawing, etched with charcoal, but every line showed her incredible talent. The subject... he arched his eyebrows at her.

"That's not how I sleep." He choked out the words, not sure if he was flattered or horrified by the fact that he was now an Alexa Kendrick original. "I most definitely do not pose like that."

Alexa laughed, the sound low and enticing. "I figured I was allowed some artistic license." Setting the sketch pad down on the windowsill, she turned fully. Her troubled expression pulled his attention from the sweet planes of her naked skin.

"I... I want to show you something. Something I don't quite know what to make of." He nodded, noting the way her shoulder shook as she sucked in a deep breath.

Bending to pick something up, she crossed the small room, perched on the edge of the bed, handing him what turned out to be a book.

"What is it?" Nate sat up fully, the sheets pooling around his waist. Bending, he reached for the bedside lamp, blinking when it illuminated a small black book. "A journal?"

"I... maybe. I don't really know." Alexa sank her teeth into her lower lip, worrying the soft flesh. "I'm asking... because you used to be a cop."

Alarm bells began to ring inside of Nate's head. Wanting nothing so much as to throw the book to the side and soothe Alexa, he still forced himself to do as she'd asked and turned back the cover.

He found himself instantly shifting into cop mode, analyzing the details of the page before he started reading.

Photocopies on generic white paper, enlarged slightly. Probably photocopies of photocopies, given the poor quality of the images.

A quick scan took him a bit deeper—the handwriting appeared male, though of course that was something that would have to be verified. There were quite a few grammatical errors, but not as many as there could have been, which indicated some schooling, but whoever had written it—and his gut told him it was a man—likely hadn't finished high school.

He went back to the beginning of the first page, this time paying attention to content as he read. The story that the words spelled out chilled his blood.

"Alexa." Setting the book aside, he reached for her hands. "This isn't about you, is it?"

"What?" She jerked her hands away, clearly shocked. "No. God no."

"Okay." Nate was hugely relieved. "Then tell me more."

Alexa hesitated, her hands fisting in the quilt, toying with the worn fabric. "I found it in the attic.,. here, and I think… I'm afraid that this might be talking about Ellie."

"Ellie." Nate frowned, trying to place the name, before realizing that Alexa was talking about her sister, the woman who owned Estelle's Blooms.

"Yes." Alexa looked at him with wide eyes, concern etched on her features. "I told her I'd been in the attic and she got really defensive. Told me to stay out of there. This is the only thing strange up there. She was hiding it, and I think it's because it happened to her."

Alexa paused, taking a deep breath. "I really don't know my sister at all. I don't know the story behind us. But she strikes me as the type of person who, if this kind of thing happened to her—she wouldn't want many people to know. Wouldn't want to seem weak."

"Right." Nate didn't remind her that victims of attack were no more at fault than anyone else in the wrong place at the wrong time. Instead he answered the unspoken question that he could see in her eyes. "Do you want me to look into it?"

"It's that simple?" Her stare searched his face, which felt as though it had been carved from stone. Only for her, he realized—only for her would he make contact with his past, with the connections that he still retained.

"I like simple." Reaching out, he pulled her to him, wrapped her in his arms. Her skin was cold, but warmed quickly beneath his touch.

"Thank you." Her words were whispered into the dark, hard to hear yet strong enough to pull at his heartstrings.

"So… you think this happened to Ellie," he started slowly, squeezing when she stiffened, then relaxed. "Then… what happened to you?"

She didn't bother to deny it. "That obvious?" Her voice was wry.

"Former cop, remember?" His palm splayed over her belly possessively, and she relaxed into the touch, leaning against him, her back to his chest.

"I already told you I was in a car accident," she started slowly. Nate did his best to stay still, not wanting to interrupt her thoughts. "If I work really hard, I can remember fragments leading up to it—for instance, I know that I went for a drink beforehand. I was celebrating a big sale, of one my paintings."

Nate stilled at this, the reminder that she was a part of another world entirely, a classy, wealthy one in which he would never fit. But as she rubbed her cheek against his shoulder and he noted how perfectly their bodies fit together, he understood that it was too late to go back.

"After that… it's blank until I woke up in the hospital. Jesus, Nate, it almost killed me. My jaw, my cheekbone, my ribs were shattered, I was sliced and diced and nearly bled out. I almost *died*. Yet I have this great, gaping hole in my memory."

Nate remained silent, not wanting to interrupt, but his arms tightened around her to show his support.

"I wasn't at fault. Jesus, I don't even know most of the details of the crash because I can't stand to read about it. But I know that I lived, and others did not. Even though it wasn't my fault, I still feel this… this guilt. This awful, dragging guilt, dragging me down every single day. Blocking me from remembering, I think."

Twisting, she looked up at him, and something clicked in his own memory. "This was in Phoenix? About a year ago?"

"Yes." Alexa nodded, her eyes questioning. "Why? Do you know something about it?"

Nate winced with sympathy at the eagerness in her voice. "I just remember seeing a news report on it. That's all. I'm sorry."

He did—a vague memory, hearing of a bad crash on the freeway just outside of Phoenix. He'd thought that there had been no survivors, but then, he hadn't paid much attention, since he hadn't yet been living here. Had been drowning in his own problems.

"Ah." Alexa sighed, as though the world was weighing her down. "Right."

"I've been floating along ever since. Not painting, living with my mother and keeping my head buried in the sand. Then Ellie showed up, and… it gave me a purpose, you know? Finding out things about a family that I never knew I had. It felt like maybe I was going to get my life back on track."

"Isn't it, though?" Nate understood, oh how he understood. It wasn't enough to just drift, no matter how badly you wanted to. Drifting allowed time for thinking, and thinking was bad for people whose minds housed demons.

Alexa shook her head. "It's stupid, I know. But I feel like… somehow I feel like, remembering my past will help me make peace with the accident. But then I found out my mother has been lying about things with my dad, and Ellie dumped the shop on me, and I found this book…" Holding up her hands, she let them fall in a gesture of helplessness. "I just don't know what to do anymore. How to feel. Who I am."

"You are who you are in the here and now. The past might help shape you, but it doesn't define you." He could just as well have been talking about himself, Nate realized with a start. "I think that if you make peace with the present, with who you are now… that's when you're going to be happy."

"You're a part of my present," Alexa said mildly. Nate waited for the squeeze of a fist around his heart—weren't men supposed to want to run and hide when women brought up relationship talks? Instead he found himself baring his teeth, ferocious at the thought of anyone or anything trying to separate them. "But how can you live in the present without wondering about the future?"

Nate clasped his hands around her waist, turned her so that she was straddling his lap. Pressing her to him until their noses, their foreheads, their bodies were touching, he savored the warmth of her breath, misting over his skin.

"Something brought us together, Alexa. And I'm not going anywhere. Not unless you tell me to."

*   *   *

WITH THE BOOK IN Nate's hands, Alexa found that she was able to relax as she made her way down to the shop the next day. That, she realized, paralleled the dynamic between them the night before.

When Nate had taken control of her body, Alexa had been free to simply *be*. While he had the book, and had promised to look into it for her, she could stop fretting about the what-ifs that the pages contained.

This meant, however, that she had room in her head to deal with some of the other issues in her life. Before she unlocked the door and started to drag the buckets of flowers outside for display, she found herself behind the counter, staring down at the cell phone that she held clutched tightly in her hand.

She reminded herself that there was no reason to be afraid—her mother was the one in the wrong here. The one who had lied.

But if she confronted Tracy—there was no going back. Their relationship would never be the same. No matter how complex that relationship was, Alexa still valued it more than almost anything else in her life.

Sucking in a breath so deep that she made herself dizzy, Alexa opened her contact list, and stabbed her finger over her mother's name.

As she listened to the ringtone on the other end of the line, Alexa felt her pulse increase, a rapidly increasing tattoo that made her feel nauseous. It was a huge relief when her mother's voicemail kicked in.

Voicemail didn't interrupt, and didn't talk over her. Yes... she could spit this out to voicemail.

"I have something to tell you," she started in a rush, not bothering with a greeting. It was her mother, after all. There was no need to introduce herself.

"I... I didn't tell you the whole truth about why I was coming to Florence. I... a woman named Eleanor Kendrick tracked

124

me down. Said she's my sister. And it looks like she's right. At first I didn't tell you because I didn't know if I believed her. But now..."

Alexa swallowed thickly, took another deep breath. "There are… things, Mom. Strange things. Like the family picture that I found. There's a date written on that back that says I was three when it was taken… but I thought Dad died when I was two. That's another thing, I'm not remembering much but… I'm getting the feeling that…"

She sucked in a breath, dread coiling in her stomach. "Did we leave before Dad died? Is he even dead?"

She paused, leaning against the counter for support. She and her mother had rarely parted without telling the other that they loved them, but right now… she just couldn't spit out the words. Instead she ended the call, then just stood there, for five minutes or an hour, she didn't know.

Had she done the right thing? Or were some things better left buried?

She didn't know. But it was done now. So she did as Nate had suggested, focusing on the present. Making her way to the front of the shop, she threw open the door and greeted a new day.

*　　*　　*

ON THE OTHER END of the line, Tracy sat down on the floor of her greenhouse, right in the midst of her orchids.

How many secrets could one person keep?

Absently, she stroked her fingers over the velvet white bloom of one of her pretties. She hoped that the touch would soothe, the way her flowers so often did, but today the hole in her heart was too big to be healed.

As a parent, every hurt inflicted on your child was echoed in your own soul. You started to hurt even before they knew they'd been wounded. So what was she to do?

As Alexa had said, there were things having heavily between them… things she'd thought Alexa would never need to know. But what was the point in knowing those things when that knowing would only create pain?

But if Alexa had discovered Ellie… there were things that the older Kendrick girl knew that the younger didn't. Things it seemed that Alexa was on a collision course to find out.

Wouldn't it be better to tell Alexa herself, before Alexa uncovered the memories on her own?

Tracy trembled as she hugged her knees to her chest. She'd allowed herself only two weak moments in her life, once after Joseph, and once when she'd seen her flesh and blood lying broken in a hospital bed.

She wouldn't weaken now.

Forcing herself to get up, she blindly made her way out of the greenhouse, down the hall and up the stairs to her bedroom. There she pulled out a box of monogrammed stationary, and the expensive pen her own father had given her at graduation.

There was so much to say, and no voice with which to say it. So Tracy put pen to paper, and began to write.

Dear Alexa…

CHAPTER ELEVEN

WITH THE BOOK IN Nate's hands, and out of her care, Alexa felt as though an anvil had been removed from around her neck. And if she tucked away her other worries, the questions about her past...

Maybe she should have felt bad. But with Nate's words ringing in her ears—the ones reminding her to live in the present...

She embraced it, as best she could. Her budding romance with a sexy as sin, brooding former cop certainly didn't hurt.

But the universe seemed to have a way of trying to make things balance... when too much went right, something had to bring it back down. So after a week in which Alexa found a groove in the flower shop, was more inspired to paint than she'd been in years, and spent her nights wrapped in Nate's arms, the downward spiral came in the form of a letter, a thin envelope covered in what she instantly recognized as her mother's handwriting.

The letter was addressed to Alexa... care of Estelle's Blooms. This made Alexa's heart rate stutter in her chest.

That Tracy had known where to send it... that alone was confirmation of so very many things. She'd mentioned that she'd found a flower shop that seemed familiar, and she'd told her mother about a family picture that she'd found.

Mailing something to Alexa care of her maternal grand-mother's shop? It was an admission. The tip of the iceberg. So, it was with trembling fingers that Alexa turned the sign to closed and locked the door, then leaned on the back counter. The envelope sliced through her finger as she eased open the flap, but she didn't notice the stripe of pain, focused entirely on pulling out the sheet of her mother's signature stationary and starting to read.

Dear Alexa,

I have started this letter half a dozen times, and can't find any elegant way to broach the subject. So forgive the bluntness, and allow me to just dive right in.

I met your father my senior year in college, at the student bar on campus, here in Phoenix. He was older, not much, but enough that I was hugely impressed by his worldliness, the fact that he'd seen things that I hadn't. He was a hippie a decade too late, one who couldn't go a day without smoking pot and railing against 'the man'. In short, he was everything that I, raised in conservative wealth and privilege, was not.

Your father was a poet, always knew just what to say, and I fell for him hard and fast. We married three months after we met, and another month after that I was pregnant... pregnant with you.

We were over the moon—I cannot tell you enough how very wanted you were, my sweet Alexa. Never doubt that.

But Joseph... Joseph's mind was not entirely healthy. Some-times it led him to do things that didn't make much sense to anyone else... things like marrying a woman, getting her pregnant, when he was already married to someone else.

To Joseph, this wasn't a big deal, because to his mind, the other relationship was over. The woman had left him, and had taken their daughter—that would be your Ellie.

But the fact that we were not legally married mattered very much to me... and to my parents. They disowned me, and you, which is why they've never been a part of our lives. People who are so cold, and who can so easily cast aside their blood... I didn't want them in your life. They didn't deserve the miracle that was you.

My parents had been our sole source of financial support—Joseph didn't want his 'wife' to work, but he didn't much want to, either. I didn't come into my trust fund until I turned twenty-five. So we found ourselves moving to Florence, where Joseph was from, and moving in with his mother. She owned a flower shop, lived in a small apartment over it. And she was a miserable old woman.

I'd already decided to leave when your father did something... unforgiveable. And to make it clear, I was taking you with me. Whatever happened, you were mine, and it was because I loved you so every much that I wanted to get us both out of there.

So you were right. Though Joseph Kendrick is indeed dead now, he wasn't when we left. When you read the enclosed article, I hope you'll understand why I felt it best to keep it from you.

There are other things we need to discuss, but for now, this is enough.

Please forgive me. I love you so very much.
Your Mother

Her father had done something unforgiveable? Alexa found herself snatching at the newsprint that had been carefully tucked into the letter. A whiff of her mother's perfume drifted out of the paper, and Alexa's heart ached, physically ached with the need to close herself in her mother's arms.

She lifted the article before she could lose her nerve.

CONVICTED KILLER JOSEPH KENDRICK DIES IN FLORENCE JAIL

No.

Surely there was some explanation.

But as her eyes scanned the article, her stomach sank with dread. Joseph Kendrick—her father—had been sentenced to life for raping and killing a young woman in the town of Florence. His attorneys had plead insanity, claiming that their client had bipolar disorder.

While the diagnosis had been confirmed, it had been concluded that he had nevertheless been fully in control of his faculties at the time of the crime.

He had been remanded to a prison in Florence—the very one where Nate now worked.

The letter from her mother fluttered to the floor, gleaming white against the forest green linoleum of the shop. Alexa wavered, doing her best not to fall over.

This—this was what her mother hadn't wanted her to know. That her father—her own flesh and blood—had been capable of something so very horrific.

A sharp pain sliced through her brain, making her cry out, bringing her to her knees. Something bright tried to punch its way to the surface of her consciousness, bringing with it so much pain that Alexa did everything she could to shove it back down.

The snippet of memory finally receded—for the moment, at least.

Alexa had no desire to remember anything from her past, not ever again.

She huddled on the floor until she grew stiff and the shadows grew long—she felt as though her blood was draining out of her body, leaving her cold and numb.

How was a person supposed to absorb this information? How had her *mother*?

Her mother. Clawing her way to a standing position, Alexa reached for her cell phone. When her mother answered, she only managed to strangle out one syllable.

"*Mom.*"

"Oh, sweetie." There was a word of grief in her mother's voice. Then a hint of control as she pulled herself together. "I take it you got my letter."

"Yes." The silence between them stretched out... and Alexa had no idea how to break it.

"Can you... can you forgive me?" Tracy's voice cracked, and Alexa listened to it with disbelief. She'd never heard her mother sound like this before.

"I don't blame you." How could she, in this situation? There was no one to blame besides Joseph himself, and her father was dead and gone, leaving a mess as his legacy.

"You don't?" Her mother's voice was hopeful. This alone would have made Alexa reel.

Tracy Cunningham was many things, but she was not

uncertain. She did not ask for forgiveness. She did not admit that she was wrong.

She did not show pain, and she never, never showed weakness.

"Of course I don't," Alexa whispered, staring down at her fingers. They were cold, like ice. So, so cold.

"I just... I need some time, Mom." Her throat hurt as she spoke. "Can you give me that?"

"Alexa..." Tracy sounded as though she was going to say something else, but didn't, instead murmuring in the affirmative.

"I love you."

"Love you, too." Alexa ended the call, threw aside her phone. For a long minute she stood there, staring into space, uncertain of what to do, what to feel, what to think.

Live in the present.

What did she need, right that moment?

The thought spurred her into action. Racing upstairs, she gathered her sketch book, a fresh box of charcoal pencils. Pulling a zippered hoodie over her T-shirt in case it rained again, she locked the shop up behind her, climbed into her car and drove.

She wasn't surprised to find herself outside the prison— the one that Nate worked at. The one that had housed her father. Climbing from the car, she stared at it, hate roiling through her, mixing with confusion to make a heavy weight in the pit of her stomach.

Propping the sketch book on the hood of the car, she let her fingers begin to move, drawing without looking down. She drew shapes—hard, unyielding blocks to represent the prison itself, crossed with the diamonds of the chain link fence. The barrier that kept the inmates in, and the rest of the world out.

When she focused on the barbed wire, she winced, and her fingers flew to her throat. She traced the raised pattern on her skin with her hand, shuddering as something—a fragment of something that was broken inside of her—pressed against her, so close to breaking through.

Did she want it to? Did she want to remember?

She shook at the thought, pushing it violently to the side and letting herself continue to draw, the need to exorcise these demons with paper and ink very nearly violent.

She was beginning to wish that she'd never come to Florence at all. Because the barriers inside of her had been damaged, and there was nothing to keep them from crumbling down. And heaven help her when she remembered everything.

Because just knowing, knowing without remembering? It was bad enough.

CHAPTER TWELVE

NATE RESISTED THE URGE to look at his watch for the millionth time. His shift today had dragged, mostly because he was counting down the moments until he could see Alexa again.

"Hey. Hey, Fury."

Nate ground his teeth together in an attempt to stem his irritation. It didn't help that the last few days he'd been tasked with shadowing Eugene Higgins.

Stark had been right—something was brewing with the inmate. It was driving Nate nuts that he couldn't figure out exactly what it was.

The man was a loner, reviled by the other inmates because of the nature of his crimes. Nate wished he didn't know even as much about them as he did.

When he'd started this job, he'd adopted a policy within himself—he only wanted to know as much as he had to in order to stay safe on the job. He knew that if he delved too deep, confined to memory some of the atrocities that the men housed within these walls had committed? He wouldn't be able to treat them the way he needed to. Because part of the job of correctional officer was not just to keep peace, but to make sure that the rights of prisoners, such as they were, were respected.

If he knew the details about the murders, the attacks, the rapes that these men had committed? He'd start making plans to bury them all alive. It was a kneejerk reaction from his years on the force... he'd spent so long mired in the dregs of society, it had become second nature to separate the world into 'us' and 'them.' He'd had the power to do away with the 'them.'

But that was no longer the case. He had to maintain some semblance of camaraderie with these men in order to ensure their compliance.

Some days were harder than others. Like every day since Eugene Higgins had decided that Nate was his best buddy, all because Nate had taken a shiv meant for him.

Nate rubbed his healing shoulder wound absently, wondering how he would have reacted had the situations been reversed. He would have felt gratitude too, he knew. But this... this bordered on the extreme. Especially since he hadn't acted for Higgins specifically—he would have done the same thing for anyone.

"Fury!"

Nate's jaw clenched. He'd been ignoring Higgins' attempts to get his attention for the last hour, maintaining that he had work to do. But maybe if he saw what the inmate wanted, it would make the last minutes of his shift tick by quicker.

"What is it?" He didn't miss the grin that spread across the other man's face when he finally, finally caught the attention of his idol. It was... eerie, the way that Higgins had focused in on him so entirely.

"I made you something." They were in the middle of recreation time, and Higgins had behaved well enough lately to have earned himself a few privileges. He'd been sitting alone at a corner table for most of the hour, alternating between trying to get Nate's attention, and focusing on his flex pen and sheet of paper.

"No gifts, Higgins." Gifts could be interpreted as bribes by the warden, and more that than, Nate wanted nothing from a man he now knew to be a rapist. Chances were that Higgins, in his twisted little mind, was using this as a levelling device, a way to bring himself up to Nate's level, or Nate down to his. To cement their 'friendship.'

Not healthy and also not wanted.

It was the flash of pure rage in Higgins' eyes when Nate refused that caught his attention, far more so than the scratchy writing that covered the sheet of paper, front and back. A chill slid down his spine, a finger of ice, and he straightened, felt himself pull on the face that he'd once used on the streets of Los Angeles—his mean-as-a-snake cop face.

"Is there a problem, Higgins?"

For the longest time, the inmate didn't respond, just locked eyes with Nate, a testosterone fueled staring contest. Though circumstances dictated that Nate would, by necessity, win, it didn't stop the unease roiling in his gut at the lack of emotion in the other man's eyes.

"No," Higgins said finally, dropping his eyes back to his paper. "No problem."

"Good." Nate stood back, ostensibly turning his attention elsewhere, but still watching the other man with his peripheral vision.

With a final glare in Nate's direction, the inmate began to meticulously fold the piece of paper, first in half, and then again and again, until it was a tiny square that he slipped into his pocket. The care with which he treated it made Nate wonder what was on it. He could have demanded to see it. But given the fact that Higgins had tried to gift it to him in the first place, it seemed like more energy than the fuss was worth when, in the end, it would probably wind up being a crudely written poem.

The buzzer sounded, signalling that rec time was over. In the bustle of escorting the inmates back to their cells, and then in the relief of his shift ending, the strange note faded from Nate's mind.

He had promised to call Alexa the second he was done. It might have been egotistical of him, but... he'd kind of expected her to answer when he called.

Instead, he was connected to her voicemail. He hesitated for a moment, decided that he didn't care if he looked like a besotted fool, and dialed again, thinking that maybe she'd been in the shower.

This time, there wasn't even a ring, which meant that she was either out of range, or had turned her phone off.

For a moment rejection settled under his skin. He didn't suffer from low self-esteem, and knew that what he and Alexa had was new but strong. But the fact remained that he was working through some hellishly big issues. They both were, and he wouldn't blame her if she bailed.

Wouldn't blame her, but he would be miserable.

Still... to just shut him out? That didn't seem like the woman he was coming to know.

But calling her a third time... that was bordering on creepy. So he tucked his cell into his pocket, got into his car, and pulled out of the prison complex.

He'd resisted the urge to call a third time, but the short drive into town was just long enough to have worry settling like a stone. Call it a gut feeling, intuition, he didn't care, but instead of heading home, he found himself parking in front of Estelle's Blooms.

It was a Monday; the shop didn't close until six. But here it was, five thirty, and the lights were off, the door locked.

Shading his eyes, Nate looked at the apartment above—a light was burning in the bedroom window, but he didn't see any movement.

Any signs of life.

"Shit." He knew he was likely overreacting—Alexa was a grown woman, and likely wouldn't appreciate his interference—but he just couldn't shake that heavy feeling in his gut. The one that told him that something wasn't quite right here.

Calling her wasn't working. On impulse, he knocked on her neighbor's door, wincing a bit when he heard a cacophony of cat noises. After what seemed to be an eternity, an elderly woman answered the door, scowling when she saw him.

"Got the wrong door, don't you, sonny?" She raised an eyebrow at him, then stopped to pick up a fat ball of fluff. Tucking said fluff under her arm, she eyed Nate suspiciously when he didn't move. "I suppose you want to know where the Kendrick girl has gone."

"She left?" Once again, the tendrils of doubt tried to grab hold of him, and once again, he yanked them out by the root. "Can you tell me anything else?"

"You know, my husband was just the same as you." The old woman banged the cane she was clasping in one hand on the floor. "You men need to learn that we women just need a break from time to time. Away from your incessant demands. Always about your needs, you men."

Nate refrained from rolling his eyes. "You're absolutely right. But in this case, I'm more concerned for her well-being than in my, ah, needs." He grimaced a bit, not wanting to dwell on that with the octogenarian.

The woman glowered at him. A second cat appeared to wind its way around her ankles, demanding attention, and she unceremoniously shoved the first one at Nate. "Here. Hold Muffy for me."

"Ah..." Nate really had no choice but to catch the white cotton puff that was launched in his general direction. It looked up at him, batted at his nose, and told him with unblinking eyes that it wasn't overly impressed with what it saw.

The woman caught the new cat up, gnarled fingers running through its fur while she stared at Nate, apparently contemplating his question. Not until the cat settled down into the crook of his arm did she nod, sniff, and reply.

"Girl piled a bunch of art supplies in her car about an hour ago. Took off like hellhounds were on her tale." The woman gestured dismissively with her hand. "If I could go back a few decades, I'd get my husband to buy a building somewhere else. Comings and goings and drama, nonstop at that place. I've had about enough of it."

"Did she... seem okay?" *He was overreacting. Totally overreacting.* But... something just didn't feel right.

The woman rolled her eyes, dropped the cat she was holding,

and grabbed the one cradled in Nate's arms. It screeched and dug in with its claws, right over his stab wound, and stars danced in front of his eyes.

"Not every woman needs a hero. You remember that. She's survived till now. She'll keep on surviving." Then the woman slammed the door in Nate's face, leaving him wondering if she was maybe, possibly, just a little bit senile.

Frowning, he returned to his car. So Alexa had taken off with her paints. He supposed that an artist might get so inspired that she just had to go create, right that second—but the Alexa he knew wasn't like that. She might have the sudden urge to go paint... but she'd make herself wait until her work day was over to do it.

Still... what was he to do? Like her neighbor had pointed out, she was a grown woman. Likely, she was fine.

But what he'd finally decided was his inner cop voice was still shouting at him, so instead of heading to the Chat 'n Chew or home, he found himself driving up and down the streets of Florence. He'd feel like a slightly obsessive, overprotective ass later, but right now, it was the only thing that soothed his jangled nerves.

He didn't see Alexa or her car anywhere in the town, and though he checked it continually, there were no calls or texts from her on his phone, either.

Dusk fell as he drove, widening his search to the area around town—the area that housed the prisons.

Still nothing.

Frustrated, feeling useless and with dread holding him firmly in its hands, he drove back to town, planning to do one last drive by of the flower shop, then head home to... he wasn't sure.

The light in Alexa's bedroom window was still on, but this time, he could see a figure moving.

Thank God.

Parking so abruptly that the tires squealed on the pavement, Nate jumped from his car and rushed at the shop. Stabbing his finger on the doorbell, he rocked back on his heels while he waited for Alexa to respond.

In his pocket his phone buzzed with an incoming text.

The door's unlocked.

Those three words meant multiple things—not only that she was waiting for him, but that she'd expected him to be looking for her. Worrying about her and yet she hadn't gotten in contact.

Grinding his teeth together against a sudden surge of anger, he opened the door—it was indeed unlocked—and made a point of locking it again behind him. The chilly air in the cooler did nothing to cool him off as he headed up the now familiar stairs, starting to speak as soon as he pushed into the apartment.

"Damn it, Alexa. I've been worried sick—" But she wasn't in the living room. Was no longer in the bedroom where he'd seen her shadow. Following the faint sound of water running, Nate cautiously knocked on the bathroom door. The lack of response had his gut twisting yet again, so he twisted the knob and slowly pushed his way into the dense cloud of heavy steam.

"Alexa?" Nate blinked against the moist air, which clung to his hair, his clothes and his skin. Then he found her, wearing nothing but one of those damn cat T-shirts, perched on the edge of the toilet, arms wrapped tightly around her torso. Beside her, scalding water roared into the enamel tub, great billowing clouds of mist rising in its wake.

Wordlessly, Alexa looked up at him. Moisture clung to her eyelashes, to the tendrils of hair that had escaped from her ponytail, and despite the heat in the tiny room, her creamy skin was white as snow. When he stepped forward, clasped her hands in his, he found that her fingers, too, were icy cold.

"Alexa. Honey. What's going on?" He made to pick her up, wrap her in his arms, but she shook her head and pulled away, which was like a knife slicing through his soul.

"This." She rasped out just the one word, gesturing with a tilt of her head to the counter. There Nate found a yellowing newspaper clipping, its edges curling from the dampness in the air.

The headline screamed out at Nate as he carefully picked up the paper, and without reading anymore, he turned to Alexa and, clasping her under her arms and behind her knees, picked her up like he would a child.

"Oh, baby." He crushed her to his chest, trying to convey with his body how very sorry he was. "Oh, baby. I am so sorry."

The feeling of his arms around her finally seemed to stir a reaction in her; she buried her face in his neck, a shudder working over her body. "I wanted to know. I came here because I thought I needed to remember."

Nate placed a kiss on the top of her head. Damn it, he wished he could take her pain inside of him, to deal with it himself. Anything would be better than the agony of watching her suffer.

"You couldn't have anticipated this." There were no magic words to make this better. Nate knew that all he could do was let her know he was here, that he had her back.

"I wanted to know," she repeated, pulling back to look him in the eyes. The despair he saw there tore his heart in two. "I wanted to know. But this... this is worse. My father raped a woman and killed her. That's in my blood. What does that make me?"

"No. Do not think like that." Shaking his head firmly, Nate shifted, sitting down on the edge of the tub, arranging Alexa so that she was on his lap, facing him, his arms wound around her tightly.

"But it does. My father is part of me. So that... what he did... that's part of me too." Alexa started to shake, an unidentifiable noise starting from somewhere in the depths of her chest. Before he could tell her how very wrong she was, the dam overflowed, and he felt her tears, hotter even than the water still cascading into the bath behind him, burning his chest.

Ignoring it, he just pulled her even closer, murmuring words meant to soothe, running hands over her hair, her back, the way one would a skittish animal. She cried as though in a pain the likes of which he'd never seen before, and Nate—a man used to action, to fixing things, felt completely and utterly useless in the face of so much grief.

When the shaking slowed, and the flow of tears lessened—and Nate thought she was capable of hearing him again—he took her chin in his hands and tilted her head so that she was looking him in the face.

"It doesn't work like that, Alexa." He continued where their conversation had left off. "The person that you are inside has nothing to do with your father. That thing that makes us who we are—our soul—that comes from someplace else. But evil? That's shaped by our flesh, by our experiences here on Earth, by our body's limitations."

Alexa looked up at Nate wordlessly, not blinking, but at least seeming to listen, which was a start. He continued, not realizing that he was repeating things that had been said to him throughout his years of Catholic schooling—things that had never really made sense until now.

"Being human can warp us. But that's a choice. So now your choice is to let what you've discovered shape the rest of your life, or to realize that it's on your father, and has nothing to do with you."

"Do you really believe that?" Alexa's voice was hoarse, as though she hadn't spoken in years. Nate sensed that his answer would weigh heavily.

He thought back to that night in Los Angeles, to the memory of the life leaving his partner's eyes. Of the young kid who had been so desperate that he'd made the wrong choice, and would spend the rest of his life paying for it.

"Yes," he said finally. "Yes, I do."

In his arms, Alexa stilled, then pushed herself in even closer to his chest. They sat still for a moment, the only sound in the room the rush of water behind them.

"I feel dead inside," she finally whispered, and he could just barely hear her. He felt as though a fist was squeezing his heart.

"I know." He did, he knew exactly. Just like he finally understood how important it was to go on living, to understand what a gift life was.

Finally, finally, Alexa relaxed in his arms. Burying her face against his chest, she seemed to be listening to his heartbeat, counting out the beats before meeting his stare.

"I'm, glad you're here, Nate. I'm really glad that you're here."

*   *   *

TRACY HAD BEEN DOING her best to maintain radio silence, to give Alexa the space she needed to digest that certain things in her life had been a lie. The problem?

There was more that Tracy needed to share with her daughter. Now that she'd removed one log from the dam, it seemed as though there was no stopping the flood.

The rest of it? She couldn't express herself via pen and paper, she needed to be there. To be a mother to her daughter when the tower of secrets crashed down onto both of their heads.

So she climbed into her car with only a hastily packed bag, and set off for the one place she'd sworn to never return to.

CHAPTER THIRTEEN

"ALEXA. ALEXA! WAKE UP."

Alexa screamed and shoved at the solid length of muscle that pressed against her. It instantly pulled away, leaving her free to claw her way up out of the sheets, heart hammering so fast she felt sick.

"Alexa." Swallowing past the sour taste of fear that coated her throat, she looked toward the sound of the voice.

Nate. Of course it was Nate. It had been just a dream, and she was here, safe, with Nate.

"I'm sorry." This time, instead of mistaking him for the dark force in her dream and shoving him away, she launched herself at him, burrowing into his arms. "God, what a nightmare."

"Do you want to tell me about it?" Pulling her into the vee of his legs, he settled her back to his front, fastening his arms securely around her waist. Letting her know he was there. As she nestled into him she felt his body react, his cock hardening against the small of her back, but he didn't make a move, reinforcing to her that she'd found a good man.

Maybe even the right man.

He didn't push her to talk, either, which was why she was able to. After taking a moment to bask in his warmth, the words that had been frozen by the icy fear in her dream thawed enough that she was able to speak.

"I think... I think I was dreaming about my accident. That's the only reason I can think of for me to be that scared." She swallowed, winced at how raw her throat felt. "Except I wasn't in a car, didn't hear anything like you'd expect—screeching tires, crumpling metal. It was just... dark. Except that I could see this line of barbed wire, stretched out across my vision." She shuddered, nestling into the comfort of Nate's arms.

"Do you think it was a memory coming back?" Nate pressed a kiss into her hair, the way he'd taken to doing—and the fact that it had already become a habit between them warmed her heart and gave her hope.

Alexa frowned at the question. "I think it must be."

But that didn't feel exactly right. There wasn't that spark of recognition, that instant relief that occurred when the brain snapped two pieces of a puzzle together. But maybe that was because the memories had been buried for so long.

On the bedside table, Alexa's phone buzzed with an incoming text. Leaning over to check it, she felt her heart sink when she read the illuminated message.

"Ellie's coming home today." She felt her stomach do a slow roll. Replacing the phone, she caught up the book that she cursed ever finding, holding it in her lap as she settled back against Nate. She'd pulled it from the pocket of Nate's coat the night before.

Twisting so that she could look up at him, she felt dread coil inside of her. "What do I do about this, Nate? The way I found it, the fact that she was defensive about me going up into the attic... my gut tells me this is about her."

Nate grimaced. "We don't know that for sure."

"Then she knows something about it," Alexa persisted, sitting up straighter, "and I know you think it was her, too. You just don't want to say so until you have more evidence."

"Old habits die hard." He ran fingers through his hair, leaving messy spikes behind. "Which is why I don't think you should say anything about it just yet."

"How can I not?' Alexa traced her fingers down the spine of the book. "Unless I go put it back where I found it and pretend that I never read it, she's going to know I found it. She's going to go check that it's there, first thing."

Nate sighed, seemed about to speak, when Alexa realized something else.

"Oh God, she doesn't know about our dad, either. She didn't even know he was dead, so I'm sure she doesn't know." Horror was red hot. "How the *hell* am I supposed to tell her that?"

Twisting in the sheets, she rose to her knees beside Nate, hoping he had an answer, but realizing that it was her decision to make.

"Remember some of what I said last night before you make yourself sick, okay?" Threading his fingers in her hair, he pulled her close for a kiss. The simple act of skin to skin contact with this man was enough to calm her.

"Worry about getting yourself through the day first, Alexa. Everything else will come from there."

Sound advice, Alexa thought as she sank into the kiss. If only she had the slightest inkling of what that 'everything else' might entail.

* * *

NATE'S SUPERVISOR WAS WAITING at the entrance of the prison when Nate arrived at work later that morning.

"Fury. The warden needs to see us in his office." The man spun on his heel, clearly in a hurry and expecting Nate to follow. Nate was more than a bit startled by this announcement.

He rarely saw his supervisor, since the man seemed to have deemed him more competent than average and felt no need to check in with him. The warden? He'd met him only once, and that by chance.

"Is there something wrong, sir?" The formality was tacked on as a habit, the way he'd always addressed his superiors on the force. He knew that Macklehenny, his supervisor, was amused by it, but Nate suspected that he also secretly liked the hint of respect that was so hard to find anywhere in this kind of a facility.

"That remains to be seen." Macklehenny's voice was brisk, and though Nate felt a twinge of anxiety, he brushed it aside quickly enough.

He knew that he hadn't done anything wrong. The anxiety came from one thought only—losing this job might mean moving, and moving would take him away from Alexa.

Not that they'd discussed the future. But he also knew that he would do anything in his power to make them work.

Macklehenny gave a quick knock on the door of the warden's office when they arrived, then proceeded to enter, Nate trailing in his wake. He was taken aback to find two uniformed police officers seated by the warden's desk.

Instinctively he felt his spine straighten, the rigid bearing of his training instinctively moving his body.

He felt the eyes of the cops on him as he followed Macklehenny into the room. He nodded once at them, then at the warden.

The female cop, whose nametag read *Preston*, eyed him up and down, making him feel a bit like a subject about to be interrogated. But she only said one thing.

"Former cop?"

He felt his lips curve up in a hint of a smile. "That obvious, huh?"

She gave him the same whisper of a smile back. "Never leaves you."

No, he thought. No, it didn't. People grew, chose new paths, and either overcame adversity or were sucked down into the mire of it, but either way, the past changed you. Influenced those decisions he'd spoken of with Alexa only the night before.

"Sit down, Fury." The warden gestured Nate toward the seat right across from him. Though Nate really would have preferred to stand, he didn't put up a fuss.

There was a serious *tone* in this office, for lack of a better word. Something was about to explode, and Nate felt like he was in an action movie, trying to run from a bomb, except he had no idea where that bomb was.

He'd just opened his mouth to ask what the hell was going on, but Preston beat him to it.

"You're probably wondering why you're here." She raised an eyebrow at Nate's look of frustration. "You're not in any trouble. At least not that we know of."

"We're just wondering if you can shed any light on this." Her partner, a massive man with skin the color of ebony, whose tag read Block, handed him a piece of paper covered by a plastic protector.

"What is it?" Nate asked, quickly taking note of as many details as he could. Cheap, generic computer paper, a little on the thin side, like the inmates were granted as a privilege. The sheet looked like it had been folded over multiple times, and had been smoothed out to be read now.

The writing on it was in blue ink, scratchy and hard to read. At the very top of one side, written in the clearly male hand, was Nate's own name, clueing him in to what this document was.

"Did Eugene Higgins write this?" He watched as Preston and Block cast a quick look at one other, communicating in that wordless way that partners did, before Preston, who had clearly been given the role of chatty cop, nodded.

"This was found last night, in a cell check. He'd hidden it in his mouth, but Officer Stark noticed that his cheek looked a little puffy." That explained the ink smears. Gross, but not surprising. "May I ask how you knew it was written by Higgins?"

Nate took another long look at the paper before returning his attention to Preston. "During rec time yesterday I was shadowing Higgins. I watched him write something long, both sides of a piece of paper. He then tried to give it to me, as a gift, I thought. I refused. He thought I wasn't paying attention after that, but I watched him fold it up into a very small square and tuck it into his pocket."

Nate cast a puzzled look at the warden. "May I ask what this is about, sir? Higgins had been allowed the paper and pen due to good behaviour."

The warden nodded, but Block cut him off. "And why would Higgins have wanted to give you a gift?" There was no censure in his tone, but Nate felt his hackles rise.

"A couple of weeks ago, there was an altercation between Higgins and another inmate in the mess hall. I intervened, and accidentally got cut by a shiv meant for Higgins." He rubbed at the healing wound absently. "I was really just in the wrong place at the wrong time, but Higgins... he took it like I'd sacrificed myself to save him. Started paying special attention to me. Like we were best friends."

Nate's eyes cut to the warden. "That's why I didn't take the paper when he tried to give it to me. I didn't want to encourage him."

The warden nodded, but again was cut off from speaking by Preston. "Why don't you take a read?"

Thoroughly puzzled now, Nate turned his attention back to the paper he held in his hand.

To Officer Fury,
I'd picked her out. I was watching her.

Invisible fingers danced over Nate's skin.

She wasn't like the other girls. She was clean and bright and the rest of them, they was all whores. That's why I wanted her so bad.

"I've read this." Nate looked up from the paper in shock, noted the equally startled looks on Preston and Block's faces as he spoke.

"I thought you said you didn't take the paper from Higgins..." Preston started, but Nate ignored her, turning back to his reading.

Yes. Yes, it was unmistakeable. The writing, the spelling and grammatical errors. Not a carbon copy, but still similar, like a person telling the same story twice over.

This paper had, beyond a shadow of a doubt, been written by the same person who'd outlined such a heinous crime in the book that he and Alexa had gone over yet again that very morning.

Which meant...

"Do you know what Higgins is incarcerated for, Officer Fury?" This was Block, who, Nate noted, was taking extra special care to note Nate's reactions.

"Rape," Nate replied hoarsely. "It's why he was attacked in the mess hall."

"Yes, rape," Block replied, disgust twisting his face. "Rape and more. He targeted a young woman, gained her trust, let her befriend him. Then he beat her into unconsciousness, raped her, beat her again, and left her for dead."

"Jesus Christ." This, *this* was why he didn't like to know the full extent of the inmate's crimes. He couldn't work among them if they knew how deeply they'd ventured into the darkness.

"He was picked up the next morning for shoplifting, and taken in when the arresting officer discovered him shoving his victim's underwear between the seats in the back of the squad car."

By this point Nate's ears were ringing. He'd heard worse, had *seen* it with his own eyes, but this...

Why was a version of this story hidden in Ellie's attic?

"He confessed once arrested, even wrote down the details. But he wouldn't give the victim's name in the confession, and even though we were able to match it up pretty quickly..."

"Is there something in here that would seal the case up tight?" Without waiting for a reply, he continued to read. When he got to the last line, he felt every cell of his body infuse with ice.

This note, addressed to him, would guarantee that Higgins would never again see the light of day. Because, in this horrible, awful recounting of the crimes of a psychopath, Higgins named his victim, and signed his name.

CHAPTER FOURTEEN

F LOWER SALES WERE SLOW in Florence that day. After arranging all the loose fresh cuts into bouquets that were, to her eyes at least, a vast improvement on her first attempts, and then bleaching every bucket in the place, along with various other chores, Alexa had succumbed to boredom. She'd settled on a stool outside the shop with her sketchpad and a fresh charcoal pencil, but nerves over Ellie's imminent arrival kept inspiration from coming.

Her fingers drifting over the snow white paper, she employed an exercise that she used when she felt blocked. Not unlike Freud's free association method of therapy, she quickly sketched anything and everything that came to mind... a banana, a hammer, a quick and dirty caricature of Channing Tatum.

Her mind drifted after her fingers lingered on Channing's stellar abs, and she found herself thinking of Nate... and from Nate, thinking of that morning in bed, when he'd held her after her nightmare.

Her nightmare. Barbed wire. Her hand began to move as she captured the image from her mind's eye on paper.

A car pulled up as she was sharpening the lines on the spikes. Thinking that it might be a customer, Alexa dusted black powder from her hands onto the thighs of her jeans before looking up from the paper.

Shock rippled through her when she recognized her mother's silver BMW. Disbelief made her feel as though she'd been yanked into a parallel universe when her normally immaculate mother stepped out of the driver's side of the vehicle dressed in yoga pants and a plain, worn button down shirt.

"Mom." Alexa slid slowly from the stool to approach her mother, caution warring with happiness. "What are you... I mean... I'm confused."

She'd told her mother she needed some time. Tracy Cunningham was a great believer in space, and it had never occurred to Alexa that she wouldn't honor that. And she'd have been pretty damn angry about it, except...

Except that Tracy looked terrible. Her skin was pale, there were purple bruises beneath her eyes. And she wasn't wearing makeup. None.

Alexa could count on one hand the number of times she'd seen her mother bare faced.

"Mom." The familiar frustration and love swamped her. "I told you. I don't blame you."

Tracy accepted the hug, but when she pulled away her lips were pressed together in a tight line. "You might after we're through talking."

"What?" Alexa's brow furrowed. "No, I really don't think I will."

"Let's go upstairs." Tracy, clearly familiar with the layout of the building, gestured to the apartment above. "I... we need to talk about something important."

A stone settled heavily in Alexa's gut, and there was no room for it, not with the one already lodged in there over what she had to tell Ellie. "Mom, today is really not a good day for this."

Her mother opened her mouth to argue, but was interrupted by another car pulling up to the curb. Alexa was swamped with the heat that she always felt upon seeing Nate when he stepped out of his SUV.

"Hi," she couldn't help but smile at him, even with the way the day had been, and even knowing that her mother was watching them. Oh, to hell with it, she thought, standing on her toes to claim a kiss—she'd deal with the maternal inquisition later.

Nate kissed her, but it tasted like desperation. Puzzled, she pulled away, noted the book in his hand, and felt a surge of panic.

"Nate. This is... ah... my mother." She stepped back, noted that Nate's eyes had already locked on the older woman. They seemed to be communicating without words, tension arcing between them in a way that Alexa didn't understand.

"Do you two know each other?"

"No." Nate shook his head.

Tracy smiled sadly. "But you know, don't you?"

Another weird silence. Alexa felt like her nerves were going to scream. She looked to Nate for an explanation, but he didn't provide her one, though the arm around her waist squeezed.

"Yes, I know. I know everything."

"Anyone care to fill me in?" Alexa asked irritably. She was damn sick of secrets. Especially since she seemed to be the only one around who didn't know them. "Like, now?"

"Let's go upstairs, baby." Nate's arm urged her toward the door of the flower shop, but Alexa stood firm.

"No, thank you. I think I'd like to know now. Right now." Her brow furrowed as she stared at first Nate, and then her mom. "The sooner, the better, actually."

"We're not doing this on the street." Always happier when she could take charge, Tracy seemed to draw herself up taller. She raised an eyebrow at Nate. "There's no going back from this, you know."

This time it was Nate who seemed sad. "She has a right to know."

Alexa groaned out loud. They were driving her insane. "Unless you're about to tell me that you two have a love child that I don't know about, spit it out."

"Not happening, babe." Without warning, Nate scooped Alexa up and hung her upside down over his shoulder. She stilled with shock before pounding on his back with her fists.

"Nate. *Not* okay!" Raising her head as best she could as Nate carried her into the shop, she looked at her mother for help.

Tracy, however, was busy, locking them in as she tucked her cell phone between her cheek and shoulder.

"Eleanor?" Her eyes flicked to Alexa's as she spoke, apology shining in her eyes. "When will you be back?" She made a few noises of agreement, and on the other end of the line, Alexa heard what she would have placed money on being her sister's voice, raised in anger.

"I'm sorry you feel that way, Eleanor. But it can no longer be helped." Tracy hung up the phone just as they all herded their way through the cooler and up the stairs, leaving Alexa limp and silent with shock.

What the *hell* was Ellie's phone number doing in her mother's phone? To her knowledge, they'd never met—her mother had only known that Joseph had had another child.

And why hadn't anyone bothered to tell Alexa *anything*?

Her heart was pounding when Nate set her down on her feet, then urged to a sitting position on the couch. She bounced right back up to her feet, ready to battle, sinking back down when she saw the weariness on her mother's face, and the sadness on Nate's.

"Please, tell me what's going on," she pleaded, looking at the man who had stolen her heart, knowing that he wouldn't lie to her. "Is it Ellie? Did you find out something about the book?"

Tracy sank into the armchair beside the couch where Alexa perched. Nate instead chose to seat himself on the coffee table. He arranged himself so that his thighs framed Alexa's, his hands could hold her own, and their faces were close.

"Deep breaths, baby," he said, before turning to look at her mother. "Maybe you should start."

Tracy nodded crisply, seemed to falter, then pulled herself back together. She looked at her daughter, and her eyes were full of grief.

"What do you remember about the time around your accident, Alexa? Has anything come back to you at all?" Tracy's eyes studied her daughter's face, searching for... something.

Alexa swallowed past a suddenly dry throat. Something was wrong here. Very, very wrong, and she had no idea what it was.

"I... no. Nothing, really." Her stare flicked helplessly to Nate. "I remember that I went to a bar, and had a drink. I was celebrating a big sale on a painting. But after that... nothing, not until I woke up in the hospital."

Tracy turned to Nate. "Why has this all come to a head now, then? I don't understand."

To Alexa's surprise, Nate pressed his forehead to hers, sucking in a deep breath—as if *he* was drawing strength from *her*.

"There was book, hidden in the attic, here," he finally said, looking back at Tracy. "Copies of letters... I'm guessing it was part of a confession. Something that the police have in their custody."

Tracy blanched. "Gabe."

Alexa looked sharply at her mother. "How do you know Gabe? How do you know *Ellie?*"

"Oh, sweetheart." Rising, her mother came to sit beside her, pulling her into a hug. Nate held her close, too, and Alexa's heart hammered against her ribs so hard she felt certain that they would crack under the strain. "I'm so very sorry."

"Mom. Nate. *Please.*" Her stare flicked from one to the other, her entire body clenching with tension.

Tracy closed her eyes for a long moment, and when she opened them again, they were wet with tears. "You were never in a car accident, Alexa."

Alexa recoiled as though her mother had backhanded her. Before she could form a word, Nate caught her face in his hands.

"Breathe. Just breathe. We'll get through this."

Dread crept down her spine, horrible possibilities whirling through her mind. But in the end, she never, never would have guessed the words that came out of Nate's mouth next.

"The book... those letters weren't about Ellie. Alexa, baby, I'm so sorry. But they were about you."

CHAPTER FIFTEEN

TIME STOPPED. FROZEN, ALEXA was frozen, her body encased in ice that would protect her from the horrible, horrible truth that she had just learned.

But the ice couldn't stand the heat of the moment, and finally, finally she was able to focus, to look at Nate, at her mother, both of whom were crying.

"I don't understand," she whispered through numb lips. "That's not possible."

Tracy rubbed her daughter's back; Alexa couldn't feel her mother's touch.

"You went out that night, like you remembered. You called me from the bar, telling me about your sale." Her mother swallowed. "You were... found... the next morning, in Sunrise Park."

"But..." It was so hard to speak, yet so important to. "How was that book here? Ellie didn't know I existed."

"She did," her mother replied, voice thick with unshed tears. "She hadn't known for long, but she knew. When she saw the article about the... about what happened to you, in the Phoenix papers, she tracked me down. Wanted updates

161

on your... condition. I... you weren't able to tell anyone details of what had happened, though we knew what... how... he had... *left* you. And then he wrote those notes for the police. I knew, but since you didn't remember... I decided not to share them with anyone. But if she had copies of those notes, then I'm guessing that Ellie got them from her husband."

Alexa couldn't breathe. And then she could, but the air hurt her lungs. "You *meant* for me not to know? To believe a lie?"

"You didn't remember." Tracy looked stricken. "The doctors said... once your brain damage had healed. They said that the memories might be lost forever, because of the damage to your head. The other thought was that they were so traumatic that you couldn't deal with them while you were healing, so your subconscious shoved them down. That they would surface when you were ready to deal with them."

A choked sound came from Nate, but Alexa's attention was on her mother.

"Either way, you didn't remember. And I couldn't see a point in telling you something so horrible, when it might keep the rest of you from healing." Tracy looked at her daughter pleadingly. "And then the months went by, and you still didn't remember, and... I just didn't know what to do."

Alexa shook her head, absolutely overwhelmed. This still didn't make any sense. "But the accident. I saw a newspaper article. It *happened*," she insisted, her brain still rejecting the notion that all of this had happened to her—was, in fact, still locked away somewhere in her subconscious.

Tracy smiled sadly. "There *was* a car accident, that same night. But you weren't in it."

Alexa started to tremble. Wrapping her arms around herself, she turned her attention from her mother to Nate. "Who? How did you... you found out today. How?"

A flicker of pain crossed Nate's face, furthering the sick sensation in Alexa's stomach.

"His name is Eugene Higgins," Nate replied levelly, his eyes locked on Alexa's. "He's incarcerated at the prison where I work."

"*What*?" Alexa recoiled, the betrayal like a jagged knife. "You... you..."

"I didn't know." Nate caught her wrists before she could shrink away from him, holding her up. "Do you hear me? I *did not know*. Not until today."

The caring, the raw empathy that was clear in Nate's voice was the final straw. Heat spilled over her cheeks, but she didn't realize that she'd started to cry until she tried to speak.

"Why?' She finally managed to spit out the one syllable. Nate tried to draw her into his arms, but she pushed them away, closing in on herself. "Why? Why did this happen?"

"There's no rhyme or reason here, Alexa." Tracy tried to reach for her daughter, without success. "You were in the wrong place at the wrong time. Just like with... with your..."

Her voice trailed off, but Alexa finished the thought in her head. *Just like with your father.*

What a cosmic joke. She was the flesh and blood of a murdering rapist. And she must have been imprinted with that, somewhere on her DNA, because she'd managed to attract one herself.

She didn't know how long she sat there, locked in the shell of her own mind. She was vaguely aware of Nate and

Tracy talking to her, to each other around her, but she'd once again encased herself in a protective shield of ice.

The noise ended when she abruptly stood, fighting her way from the tangle of well-meaning arms.

Putting a safe distance between herself and... *them*... she hugged her arms to her chest. "I need to be alone right now. I need you both to go."

"I don't think that's such a good idea—" her mother started, but Alexa shook her head violently, desperation making her lash out.

"I said *get out*!" Her voice rose to a shriek, echoing off of the walls. "Get out! Get out! Get *out*!"

Spinning, she ran down the short hall to the bathroom, where she slammed the door hard enough to make the walls shake. Locking it behind her, though she knew that wouldn't keep out anyone determined, she began to shake, violent tremors that wracked her body as she collapsed back against the door, sinking down to the floor as her legs gave out.

She couldn't think. She couldn't handle this. She was splintering into pieces.

Crawling across the tiled floor, she heaved herself onto the ledge of the tub. She turned the hot water on full, and didn't bother with any cold. Like when she'd found out about her father, she hoped that the heat, the steam would help to thaw the icy shell that had surrounded her heart, but if anything, the moist air kissing her face only made her feel colder.

When the level of the water rose close to the edge of the tub, she slid in. Her jeans were heavy, her T-shirt bloated with air, neither providing a barrier against the nearly boiling water. It hurt, it was too hot, but finally she felt something, she felt pain, and so she stayed in the bath, reaching for the white heat, until she couldn't bear it any longer, and she screamed. The scalding water cascaded over the lip of the rub, and she continued to scream, wordless sounds of anguish as the damn of her emotion broke, and all she felt was *pain.*

She heard banging at the door, heard Nate's voice, was vaguely aware of him pounding his way through, of her own voice shrieking at him to get out.

He ignored her, pulling her from the tub, ignoring the cascading water as he ripped the steaming clothes from her body, cursing as he burned his own hands. And though her skin steamed as it frantically tried to release heat, still she shook, because while she still didn't remember, now she *knew.* She knew what filled that great gaping hole in her memory, and wished she could go back to blissful ignorance.

She was vaguely surprised to see Tracy wading into the bathroom behind Nate. Her brow furrowed as her very proper mother slogged through the water to turn off the tap. When she turned, her grief filled eyes meeting Alexa's, there was no judgment about the fact that a man she'd never met before today was wrapping her naked baby girl in a towel.

"I'll clean this up," Tracy said quietly, nodding at Alexa. "I think Nate can take care of you the best right now."

Alexa frowned, since something about that wasn't right... Tracy wasn't the type to hand over control. She should have been right in there, trying to force Alexa back to the land of the living.

Part of Alexa understood that it was because her mother loved her, that she was letting go.

Her screams quieted. The tears started to dry, though she

was a raw, seething mass of hurt and ugliness, both inside and out. She stopped shoving against Nate, going limp as he set her down on the bed, gently dried off her skin and assessed the damage the overly hot water had done to her skin.

"You're lucky." His eyes flashed with anger as he stood and pointed a finger at her. "I'm going to look for some salve for this. Don't move."

Why was he upset with her? Didn't he understand that she was broken?

She didn't care. In fact, she wasn't even sure that she was still in her right mind, she felt so very far away from reality as Nate returned and knelt at her feet.

Slowly, methodically, he began to rub ointment into her skin. Earthy lavender and maybe a hint of mint drifted to her nose, soothed the most jangled of her nerves, and provided a blessed coolness to her boiled skin.

His eyes met hers again as he rose up to smooth the cream over her shoulders, and she understood that he was, in fact, upset with her.

"If you ever pull a stunt like that again, I will spank you so hard you can't walk for a week." His mouth pressed together in a tight line even as her own lips parted in surprise. And yet his hands were unfailingly gentle as he reached for the over-sized shirt that she slept in, pulled it over her head, and urged her arms in like she was a doll.

She let him, feeling her first trickle of relief when he smoothed the snarls of her wet hair away from her face and urged her to lie down on the bed.

She waited until he'd stripped, climbing into bed behind her. Pulling the quilt over them both, he pulled her against him, her back to his front, letting his warmth and the solidness of his frame steady her.

She felt like she should speak, but she had no words. Yet she suddenly wanted desperately to thank him for staying, for not letting her push him away, for not leaving her alone.

A strangled cry escaped her throat as she tried. And what came out was not what she intended to say.

"I don't want to remember anymore." Her throat was raw. "But I am. Like a... like a broken dam. And it hurts."

"Baby." Nate's arms tightened around her, but he didn't push, instead just letting her know he was there.

Her fingers went to her neck, trailed the raised lines of scar tissue. "Barbed wire. He used barbed wire around my neck."

Her voice cracked, and she again felt tears come streaming down her cheeks. Nate gathered her against him, stroked her, soothed her, held her as she grieved. He didn't speak until she was quiet again, and when he did, she felt her first spark of hope—maybe, just maybe, she could survive this, so long as she had him at her side.

"Let it out, Alexa. You don't have to be strong right now." He squeezed her tightly. "I've got enough for us both. And you can borrow some of mine, until you find your own again."

*   *   *

"DON'T GO."

Nate was pretty sure that Alexa didn't know she even uttered the words, floating as she was on the edge of sleep.

He wasn't going anywhere—couldn't have torn himself away if he tried. He needed to be here, with her, reassuring himself over and over again that she was whole, that she was alive.

As her breathing evened out, and her body finally relaxed in his arms, he allowed himself to sink down into the mattress. This situation was in no way about him, and yet his own emotions had been through the wringer in the last few hours.

Never, until the day he died, would he forget the look on Alexa's face when she understood that the entries in that damn book had been about her.

Hell, he would never forget how he had felt when he'd finished that note from Higgins. It was a great cosmic joke, or maybe the fingers of fate, that had orchestrated all the little connections between Higgins and himself, Higgins and Alexa. Hell, even the parallels between Higgins and Alexa's father.

The heat of Alexa's grief and rage had burned his own away—it was inconsequential in the shadow of something so huge. Not that he wasn't entitled to feel what he felt, more that his perspective had shifted.

He gathered her closer to him, needing to reassure himself that she was still there. Still breathing.

Earlier that day, when he'd finally understood the truth—understood that Eugene Higgins, the inmate who thought Nate was his best friend, had tried to kill his woman, had left her for dead...

He'd been out the door of the warden's office, blind with rage, before he'd been able to draw his next breath. It had taken both Block and Preston to hold him back.

He'd worked through his rage because he'd known Alexa would need him to. But next time he saw Higgins...

It was probably best if he never saw the inmate again.

For now, though... for now he would just hold Alexa tightly in his arms. Would be there when she needed him. And if nothing else good came from this godawful day...

Understanding that he could have lost her before he'd ever met her? It made the short length of time that they'd been together inconsequential.

He loved this woman. He was hers, as much as she was his.

And he was never going to let her go.

CHAPTER SIXTEEN

S WALLOWING THE LAST SWEET *mouthful, Alexa set her empty glass on the top of the bar, where it promptly adhered itself to the brownish flecked surface, with what, she didn't want to know. A hand reached towards it, releasing a shiny stream of quarters.*

The hand was almond brown, skinny and unhealthy looking, and had a tattoo in the fleshy part between thumb and forefinger. Dark spikes, inky lines—barbed wire.

It seemed to come alive in the dim, dancing lights of the bar. It was creepy, and Alexa moved instinctively away from its owner. Well, she tried to, but bodies crowded so heavily around her, against her, that she didn't actually move as much as she'd have liked.

The man looked hurt that she'd tried to move away. Always the peacemaker, even though this was her night, she squashed the weird jumble of feelings that were roiling greasily around in her belly and worked up a smile.

"Sorry. I... uh... you just startled me." She laughed, a shaky sound that would have fooled no one had it not been sounded underneath the harsh shrieks of the band's lead singer.

He smiled, revealing a prominent gap between his two front teeth. Somehow that imperfection endeared him to her, just a bit.

"Not much room to move in here. I'm just tryin' to see if I've got enough for a beer." He resumed counting out his quarters, adding dimes and nickels to the pile when he ran out of the bigger silver at three dollars and twenty five cents.

Alexa still felt a trickle of uneasy remorse undulating over her skin, but it made her feel guilty, so she reached into the tight pocket of her torn, faded blue jeans. Extracting a crisp ten dollar bill, she dropped them beside his somewhat pitiful pile of change.

"Here. Let me buy you a beer." She smiled up at him, the expression still not entirely genuine, because she was still kind of uncomfortable, but instead of an answering upturn of the lips, he scowled fiercely.

"I don't need no charity. You hear me?" Eyes narrowed to beady jet slits, he scraped his change off of the bar, intending, she thought, to take it and move elsewhere in the room.

She should have let him. She was here to celebrate her own success. But... wasn't this part of going out, of being young? Meeting new people?

And the guilt wouldn't let her leave it alone.

"No!" Reaching out, she clasped her fingers around his upper arm, surprised at the chill of his skin in the room that was heated with the crush of warm, hormone-riddled bodies.

He looked down slowly, looked at her spread fingers, icy pale against the russet of his skin, and looked at her curiously.

She realized that he thought she was hitting on him.

"No!" Well, crap, that hadn't come out right, either. She blamed it on the alcohol—she'd only had one glass of wine, but she wasn't much of a drinker.

"I just meant—I feel like I'm being rude. I just want to buy you a drink. That's all." Inhaling deeply enough to make her lungs sting,

she added a bald faced lie, because she felt sorry for the guy who didn't even have enough money to buy a beer on a Saturday night. "Plus I got paid today. Money's meant to be spent, right?"

And she had indeed gotten paid. It was why she was here, celebrating her first six figure sale.

The stranger slowly moved his stare back up from where her hand had touched, and, after a long moment in which he seemed to be considering things, nodded once, slowly.

Alexa grinned with relief, though why she was relieved that he was letting her buy him a beer when she suddenly wanted desperately to go home, she wasn't quite sure. She placed their order—another glass of sweet white wine for her, and a bottled, cheap brand of beer available by the truckload for him.

She thought it was kind of nice that he hadn't ordered something super expensive on her dime.

"So." Alexa felt incredibly unsure of what to do. She'd only bought him the drink because he'd stirred some sort of pathetic pity in her heart.

Before she could open her mouth, he pulled up the sleeve of his dingy t-shirt, revealing an arm with skin stretched painfully tight over ropy muscles, tightly enough that she could make out the network of veins—fat, blood swollen tubes. The chestnut membrane was decorated with more of those eerie strands of barbed wire, those long, somehow elegant swooping lines, etched painfully deep with obsidian ink.

She grimaced before she could stop herself. The markings looked crude and primitive, somehow not as clean as they could have been. She'd seen other people with tattoos before—had even wistfully imagined getting one herself, something beautiful and prismatic.

These looked—cheap. Rough. Kind of scary.

Alexa bit her lip, sure that he was about to get mad again.

Instead, he smiled, a long slow upturning of his lips. Like he'd enjoyed her reaction—appreciated her fear.

Without another word, he dropped his sleeve. Lifting his beer, he drained the entire bottle in a series of chugs, his Adam's apple bobbing in a grotesque dance.

There was a film of frothy foam on his lip when he was done.

That foam endeared her to him again. Okay, he might have been a little lacking in the social skills department, but was he really that bad a guy? He clearly just wanted some company.

Would it kill her to have another drink and a conversation with him?

He thanked her when she ordered him another beer, coming across as a little surprised and even kind of grateful, which—she couldn't lie—boosted her own feeling of self worth a bit. She wasn't alone in that feeling, she knew—everybody did it. A little act of what people considered charity, and they'd live off the resultant buzz for a month.

"I'm Eugene." Abruptly, the stranger stuck his hand, the one with the webbing, in front of Alexa's face.

Though she didn't really want to touch that dark meshwork, she made sure that she clasped his hand firmly in her own. It was dry and cool, almost dusty feeling. She didn't want to look to check, but she felt the imprint of several raised lines pressing tight against her own smooth palm, and was sure that he had some bad scars marring his flesh.

"Alexa." Easing her hand out of his own, she took another sip of her wine, the golden liquid coating her suddenly scratchy throat rather than rinsing away grit and refreshing.

There was something… well, at the risk of sounding completely weird, something darkly sexual in his touch. Something that slithered out of his very pores, sinuous and supple enough to twine around her tightly, leaving her gasping for air.

173

Though she couldn't say that she responded to it, she could certainly feel it. She wasn't sure that she found it offensive, either—it was just... different. Stronger than anything she'd ever felt any other member of the opposite sex emote in her direction.

"Alexa." He rolled the three syllables around on his tongue, appearing to savour them like she'd wanted to savour the wine that now tasted a bit sour in her mouth. "Alexa. Pretty name. Pretty girl."

Wariness shot into her eyes, she was sure it did, powered by a small, uncomfortable clenching of her gut.

She didn't want him to hit on her. She was really bad at rejecting anyone. Hated making anyone feel poorly about themselves.

Again, instead of reverting to the hint of temper that he'd shown her earlier, he smirked, again revealing those less than perfect, somehow captivating teeth.

"Can't blame a guy for trying." Alexa couldn't see his face then, hidden as it was by the beer bottle. "'Specially when you got a mug like mine." Setting down his second empty bottle, he twisted the skin of his face into a grotesque caricature, making her laugh.

An awkward silence followed that laugh, instead of the ease that she'd thought would come.

Suddenly, she'd had enough. She'd celebrated enough, thank you very much. She wanted her bed, not the strained conversation of some guy that she couldn't figure out and who kept her on edge.

So she counted out some change to tip the bartender, lining it up painstakingly next to their empty bottles and glasses. She thought that she saw Eugene frown, just a slight glimpse of his face altering drastically from a smile out of the corner of her eye as she untied her cardigan from her hips and slid it onto her arms, but by the time she'd turned back to him his face was clear as sunshine after the rain.

"I'd better get going." Alexa offered a smile. "It was nice meeting

you." She wasn't sure that *nice* was the exact word that she should have used, but it had certainly been interesting.

"Wait. You walking?" Hastily, he donned his faded black denim shirt over the t-shirt that had been equally bleached of color. "I'll walk with you for a bit."

She didn't want him to—she wanted to be free of the incessant need to think of something to say. But he looked so eager, again seeming so excited to just have someone to talk to, that she acquiesced, leading the way out of the dim, sticky, heated bar.

What was she going to go home to, anyway? An empty apartment, her Kindle, a tuna melt? Things that she liked, certainly, but not much of a way to celebrate—all alone.

And right now she wasn't alone. She had company, even if it wasn't the kind of company she was used to.

Besides, what would it look like if she said no?

*   *   *

VOICES CUT THROUGH THE soundless air, jolting Alexa out of the black that she was drowning in. She flinched, or at least she did in her mind, because she couldn't move. She couldn't move anything. She was glued to the ground where she'd been dropped like a lifeless doll, adhered to the leaves and twigs and dirt with something that felt warm and thick like fresh made jelly, and smelled like the blood that she knew it was.

Oh please God. Please, let it be over. Please don't let him be back.

The voices were female, though, female and slightly hysterical. She felt hands patting at her, rubbing over her cold, sticky skin, pressing at the pulse under the curve of her jaw and at the juncture where her hand became her wrist.

175

Talking, talking, all the time talking, but she didn't know what they were saying. Like she no longer spoke the language of her birth.

Something warm and heavy was placed over top of her, pressing against her, but it was pleasant, not at all like the feeling of his flesh undulating on top of her own. It helped to warm her, a bit, though she truly felt that she'd never be warm again. Not truly warm—not warm and safe.

Alexa wanted to protest when her eyelids were pried open, when the crusted matter there was cracked wide and her fragile orbs were subjected to the blaring white light of what appeared to be early morning.

Was it the next morning? Was it a week later?

She had no idea.

Was she even alive?

She didn't know that either.

She could feel her pupils pulse, adjusting against the sudden influx of light. She could see colors—great swatches of grass green, of pale, pale blue. Jagged spears of white tipped grey that cut the blue to ribbons, and fuzzy ovals of moving pink and cream that refused to stay in one place.

The pressure on her eyelids was removed, and she was allowed to lapse back into the blessed dark. Before she could entirely slip away though, could escape entirely from the brutal reality of sensation, she heard a voice.

Heard and understood it.

"It's going to be okay. Do you hear me? It's going to be okay."

She didn't understand. It would never be okay again.

* * *

"IT DOESN'T LOOK GOOD."

Alexa didn't understand.

Whose voice was that? It wasn't one she knew. And why couldn't she see? Why was the entire field of her vision an implacable, grim landscape of slate, stretching as far as she could see every which way?

"Rapid papillary dilation, oculus dextra only... no wait, oculus sinistra also."

Huh?

Thoroughly confused, she struggled to sit up, to open her eyes. Why was she lying down? Had she been asleep? She wasn't even tired.

Nothing happened. Annoyed, Alexa commanded her brain again to move her arms, her legs, to crunch her abdominal muscles in a sit up. To force the ever quickening flutter of nerves in her eyes to open.

Nothing.

Panic snaked its way into her consciousness, an oily sickness in her gut. It roiled in her stomach like an over-rich meal as she frantically tried to understand why her limbs weren't working.

"Heart rate's increasing." Alexa heard, as if from a great distance, a long, repetitive string of shrill beeps, quickening irregularly before slowing again.

A flash of light, nougat yellow, registered in her right eye, then her left. She opened her mouth to protest, but instead of her own voice, she heard the lower, more moderated tones of a man.

"No pupillary response oculus unitas. Reflexes?" A sharp tap on each knee.

She was getting annoyed. She wanted to wake up.

As the minutes ticked by, however, realization slowly trickled in, water filling a vase full stones.

This wasn't a dream. This was real.

Alexa tried again to speak, and again and again. There was no sound besides the one reverberating off the shadowy confines of her mind.

She was screaming, but it seemed that no one could hear her.

She howled until even her inner voice was hoarse. As she quieted, her mind—her only companion, it seemed—turned over what she'd heard, what she'd experienced since 'waking.'

She was in a hospital, or something like that. If they were testing her reflexes, then why couldn't they see her responses? Why couldn't they tell that she was awake, just unable to speak, to see, to ask?

"Any word on an ID yet?" Another male voice, this one lighter and somehow more smooth.

"No. The patient had no identification on her. No purse, no wallet, not even a credit card."

Wait a minute. That was wrong. Completely wrong. Alexa never went anywhere without her purse, a small piece of battered leather that she'd had for years.

And patient? Patient of what? Why did she need to be here?

What had happened to her?

"What do the cops say?" This came from a woman whose voice reminded Alexa of the burnt ochre and gold sunrises at home. Home, yes, home. Was she home?

No, that wasn't right. She had her own apartment now. She loved it. She loved freedom. Love painting. Loved life until...

Until what?

Bearing down internally, she tried again, with all of her strength, to spit out the words that were choking her.

She just wanted these strange people to realize that she was awake, that she could hear them. She didn't want them to keep poking her flesh, shining lights into her eyes, or strapping monitors to her skin.

Why couldn't they hear her? Why couldn't she talk?

And what was that haze of red that was wafting on in, the curling tendrils ominous in their undulating shades of scarlet, crimson and claret?

It was—oh, God. The pain. The pain. Like a million tiny, deathly sharp blades, not stabbing but slicing, all at once, through every single bit of her flesh. Melting on through layers of derma and fat, muscle and bone.

As her breath caught, rasping painfully in her inexplicably swollen throat, Alexa heard the faint, staccato song of the beeps again. They raced, faster and faster, before pausing once, twice and slowing, sliding towards silence. She tried to shut out the pain, to breathe through it, but still she heard the busy bee hum of panicked voices, of shouted words, of things she didn't recognize.

A sharp sting in her right hand, then a lovely cool began its slow trickle, heavy and so fat with wet that it dampened the pain, bit by bit. Numbed the senses.

With its arrival the desire to speak, to yell and scream her existence, faded. She no longer cared about why she was where she was, or who was around her. Didn't care why she was trapped, an active mind in a body that wouldn't respond, no matter how loud she screamed.

Didn't care that her thoughts were decidedly hazy, disappearing like smoke in the sun.

Oh, that cool. So thick and sweet, deadening her veins and everything that they touched.

She didn't want... she couldn't... she needed to...

It all faded to grey.

*   *   *

ALEXA WOKE UP IN the early hours of the morning, shuddering and gasping for breath. The pale light of an early morning sky filtered in through the open window as she clawed her way across the covers to Nate, cold tears spilling soundlessly down her cheeks.

Waking instantly, Nate opened his eyes, took one look at her face, and opened his arms. Soundlessly, Alexa moved in, huddling against him, every part of her icy cold.

His arms were strong around her as, finally, her body relaxed and she drifted back into a fitful sleep.

*   *   *

AND SO IT WENT, days drifting into nights, drifting into days. Alexa ate when she was fed, bathed when Nate nudged her into the shower, slept more than was healthy.

But bit by bit, she began to feel more... normal. Not like the person she'd once been, but... better. Life was going on, never mind that she didn't want it to.

She tried her best to avoid her mother, not sure how she felt about being lied to in such an extreme fashion. But Tracy refused to return home, instead renting a small condo in town, bringing food and books and anything else she could think of to entice her daughter back into the land of the living.

This was an interesting turn of events, because the one decision Alexa had been able to make, was to stay in Florence indefinitely. She'd made the decision on her own, and in another strange twist of fate, overheard Nate on the phone the very next day.

"No, Hannah. I'm not coming back to Los Angeles." By now, Alexa knew what had happened to cause the shadows in Nate's eyes. A few more minutes of eavesdropping, and she understood that Nate was speaking with the widow of his former partner.

"No. This is for real. I have a new home." A pause. A definite smile in his voice. "Yes, there's a woman."

She would never have asked him to stay for her. And she would never have imagined that he would want to, not after what he'd seen of her since her world had shattered.

But understanding that not only had he stayed through her lowest low, but that he still wanted her? Wanted her enough to stay here?

It wasn't the entire reason that she started dressing herself in the morning, started feeling hungry for food, for conversation, for life.

But it definitely helped.

The shattered memories came back, bit by bit, day after day, often with frustratingly huge gaps in between. They were hard, and they made her wake up screaming in the night, but Nate was always there, arms and heart open wide.

Alexa had been aware, on some level, that Ellie and Gabe had indeed returned home the day that she'd discovered the truth of everything. She also knew that Nate and Tracy had kept her sister away until she was able to deal with it. But sometime after she started to feel better, Ellie managed to sneak up the stairs to the apartment.

"Oh, Alexa." Ellie stopped just inside the living room, her eyes wide as she took in the other woman.

Alexa, not expecting the chance meeting, just stared. She

was not prepared for Ellie to bound across the room and hug her tightly.

"This is all my fault. I never should kept that damn book." Ellie continued to squeeze, the warmth finally melting the stiffness n Alexa's limbs. "I never should have tracked your mother down in the first place."

"Don't." Alexa still wasn't speaking much, and her voice sounded hoarse. "It's... I think I'd rather know."

And that was something she was coming to understand. Hard as it was, she knew that eventually she'd been happier, having worked her way through the darkness to the other side, rather than wondering what was missing inside of her.

"Why did you want to know so badly in the first place?" This, Alexa had yet to understand. Ellie had, by her own admission, just barely found out about Alexa's existence when the accident had occurred. She didn't quite understand what had driven her sister to look up Tracy and, more, to badger copies of Eugene's confessions from her husband.

Ellie cast her a strange look. "We're family."

Alexa felt her heart sink. "Our father was family, too."

Sparks flew from the older woman, and Alexa understood that Ellie knew—Tracy must have told her.

"Family are the people who stay." She looked Alexa in the eye, nodded determinedly.

Alexa turned that over in her head. The people who stayed—that was an interesting definition. And, she thought, so very true.

It had been a week, or perhaps a week and a half, since she'd found out about Eugene Higgins. The worst week of her life. And yet the people who mattered to her—they were still here.

Her mother, though they had some issues to work out. Ellie, though they barely knew one another.

And Nate. Dependable, wonderful, sexy Nate. The rock she could cling to when the storm threatened to knock her down.

"What... what are your plans now?" Ellie cared, she knew, but Alexa also figured the other woman would be interested in knowing when she could open her shop again.

It meant a lot that Ellie had agreed to keep it closed, to stay away and give Alexa some space.

There was only one answer. "I'm staying." Why, apart from Nate, she still wasn't sure—shouldn't she want to be as far away from Eugene Higgins as possible?

But she had a sister here, one that she'd like to get to know. She'd done more painting here than she had anywhere else in the last year.

More than that, though... it just felt like where she needed to be, like the place where she could heal.

"Do you have a place to stay yet?" Ellie asked carefully, and Alexa jolted. She hadn't thought that far ahead. In fact, she'd kind of just assumed that she'd remain living here.

"I'm sure I'll find something," she finally replied. She didn't want to move. She was comfortable here. And the thought of any more big life changes at the moment made her skin crawl.

Either her feelings showed clearly on her face, or that was what Ellie had already wanted, because her sister looked at her with knowing eyes, and smiled faintly. "You can stay here, if you want. Estelle was your grandmother, too... it's only fair."

"Wow." Alexa had known that, of course she had known that... but the fact hadn't really sunk in until Ellie had said that. "Thank you, Ellie. Really."

Yet another tie to Florence. The roots of her family might be dark and twisted in places... but they were still her roots.

"Will Nate be moving in with you?" Alexa noted that Ellie was looking at her very carefully. She deliberately kept her face impassive.

"I... I don't know." And she hated the fact that she didn't know.

He had, in fact, been living here since that horrible, awful day. But Alexa hadn't thought about whether it was permanent or not.

Probably it wasn't. Moving in together, officially moving in together—that would be insanity after the short amount of time that they'd known one another.

But Nate had seen her at her worst, and he was still here.

And Alexa now understood that life was too precious, too easily snatched away, to not grab what you wanted, to hold on tight and never let go.

"You know what? I'm going to go find out." Alexa stood abruptly, dusting her hands on the thighs of her jeans. The sudden movement made her dizzy—she hadn't been moving much at all the last week.

"Nate's downstairs with Gabe." Ellie's eyes sparkled as she gave her sister a thumbs-up. "Go get 'im."

Alexa rolled her eyes, but inside she was grinning. Was this what it felt like, to have a sibling? Someone to tease you, but who ultimately had your back?

She thought she liked it. She knew she wanted more time to discover for sure.

"I'll be right back." But right now... she had a mission. A purpose. And she was going to see it out, even if she had to crawl down those stairs.

CHAPTER SEVENTEEN

F OR THE FIRST TIME in over a week, the front door to Estelle's Blooms was propped open, and buckets of flowers were outside in the sun. Alexa noted that Ellie had been busy that morning, replacing what was surely a cooler full of dried out stems with a fresh delivery.

Gabe was standing behind the till, ringing in a customer. He smiled at her as she slowly, shakily, pushed her way out of the cooler.

Nate had been leaning against a shelf full of vases, but the second he saw her, he stood up straight. She held out her hand to indicate that he should stay there, then made her way through the small shop, feeling surer on her feet with every step.

"Hi," Nate said as she approached the door. The sunlight called to her and, stepping outside, she turned her face up to the sky and drank it in.

With her eyes closed, she felt rather than saw him come up behind her. Before he could pull her into his arms, as he always did, she turned and regarded him with serious eyes.

"Is something wrong?" He looked alarmed, and Alexa

couldn't quite hold back a chuckle, the first time she'd felt like laughing in a while.

"Depends," she answered slowly, trying to keep her expression blank.

"On what?" He moved to stand in front of her, shading her eyes from the sun.

"Depends on whether or not you're going to officially move in with me." Her stomach did a flip-flop as she took in the startled expression that crossed his face.

He was shocked? Well, too bad. She wasn't backpedalling. He could take it or leave it.

"You're staying, then?" Nate's voice sounded suspiciously tight, and she eyed him warily.

"Yes." She drew the one word out into several syllables. "Right in this apartment, in fact. What did you think I was going to do?"

She watched as he huffed out a deep breath.

"I thought that you might want to get away from here." He regarded her thoughtfully. "Away from Arizona. Just... away."

"Away from you?" She wanted to flinch, then gave herself a mental smack. If this man hadn't been scared away by what had happened in the last week, then she was pretty sure he was here to stay.

She couldn't help being a bit nervous, regardless.

"You can try." Nate's response was quick and not a little feral, making her grin internally. "Wherever you were going, however much time you needed... I would have gone with you and given it to you."

He reached into his pocket, and suddenly Alexa felt frissons of nerves skating over her skin—and unlike so much of what she had been feeling lately, these one were light as champagne, frothy and oh so sweet.

"But your decision just means that I get to give you this sooner." When Nate's hand withdrew from his pocket, it was holding a small blue velvet box.

Alexa looked from it, to Nate, and back to the box. She wanted to throw out a snappy remark, but her mouth and throat had gone utterly dry.

When she again looked up, she found Nate watching her carefully through narrowed eyes.

"Wha—what's that?"

He took her hands, twined his long fingers in her own. And when her big, sexy former cop dropped down to one knee in front of her, Alexa felt her own knees wobble.

"Like I said, I was prepared to hold onto this as long as I needed to." The sunlight glinted off of Nate's hair, his eyes as he solemnly looked up at her. "But truthfully, I bought it after the first time we made love. We hadn't known each other very long—we still haven't. But when I was inside of you, when I had you in my arms, I just thought... there she is. The piece that I've been missing."

Tears welled up in Alexa's eyes, but these ones were happy. "Nate. Nate. I don't know what to say."

"You don't say anything yet. Let me ask the question, woman."

Alexa felt the laugh bubble out of her, but kept her expression down to a smirk.

"I'm not going back to the prison." Nate told her, his expression darkening for a moment. "I can't. I'll kill him. And more blood isn't the answer. But Gabe wants a deputy. I think that's what I would do... if we stayed here."

"If?" She ignored the allusion to Higgins. He had no place in this moment. No place in her new life.

"It's up to you." Nate chose that moment to open the velvet box. The ring inside caught the sunlight, sparkling in a rainbow of colors. "We're bound, you and I. I think we have been since the moment we met. As long as I'm with you, I'll be happy. I don't care where that is."

"*Nate.*" This man was so many things. A cop, a prison guard. A demanding lover and a gentle man. Rough around the edges, with the soul of a poet.

She couldn't imagine being happy with anyone else. Sucking in a breath, she waited for him to ask the question... so that she could scream yes, before he realized what a damaged woman he was binding himself to.

Except, of course, he already knew that. Already knew, and loved her just the same.

The silence stretched out, and Alexa was finally forced to let out her breath. She glared down at Nate, who not so successfully stifled a laugh and pulled the ring from the box.

"Even after a few days, I knew that diamonds didn't suit you. They're cold. And you—you're the bright spot in my world. A rainbow in a sea of grey." His clever fingers held the ring up to the light, and Alexa was all the more dazzled, knowing the thought he'd put into it. "When I saw this, I knew it was for you. It's supposed to be something called a family ring, with birthstones for the parents and the children, but I had them add a stone in the colors of the rainbow."

A family ring. Alexa thought of Ellie's comment earlier. *How perfect.*

"Family are the ones who stay." Tears started to well up as

she fell to her knees, held her hand up in Nate's face, and waved it excitedly. "Mine. Put it on. Now!"

Nate laughed, long and hard, as he slid the ring onto her finger. "I love you, Alexa Kendrick. We're family now. We're going to stay."

"I love *you*, Nate Fury." Alexa whispered back, letting his light lift her from her own darkness. "Wherever we go, that won't change."

And in that moment, the hole that had been inside of her for the last year was filled, not with horrible memories, or with trauma, but with love.

Nate had indeed lent her his strength for a little while, and she had no doubt that she'd need it again, as she continued to heal. Two broken halves, making a whole.

No, not anymore.

Two whole people...

But two people who were better together.

UNSPOKEN

Prequel to UNTOUCHED

A S ELLIE KENDRICK DROVE slowly down the narrow strip of asphalt that led to her destination, the ten years that she had been gone slowly evaporated into the dry Arizona heat.

The shop stood at the end of the block, a square structure of crumbling grey brick that sat apart from its neighbors. The wooden sign on the front of building had never been particularly bright or eye catching, but now it—and the dull brick walls—looked like a photo that had sat out too long in the sun.

Pulling her rental sedan to the side of the road—always plenty of parking to be had in Florence, Arizona—Ellie stepped out of the car that smelled like vinyl upholstery and industrial strength cleaner, and into her past.

The street was empty as she approached the door, her low heels clicking on the cracked sidewalk. Late evening in Florence meant shift changeover at the prisons had just finished, with half the town facing a long dozen hours inside a cement block, the other spending precious time with their families, eating their dinners, showering off the desert dust, crawling into bed.

Ellie traced her fingers over the letters of the faded sign, once coral over turquoise blue. Estelle's Blooms had been meant as a bright spot in town, or so Ellie's grandmother had always said.

Now, it looked like nothing so much as one of those black and white photographs that someone had tried to liven up with splashes of artificial color. Nothing real remained, and it would be so easy for Ellie to get back in her rental car, to escape the way she had so many years ago.

Of course, then she hadn't had a choice. Just, she supposed as she jingled the weight of the heavy, old key in her hand, as she didn't really have much of one now.

Ellie sighed and tucked a wayward strand of her reddish gold hair behind her ear. It flopped back exactly where it had been before she'd moved it, hanging listlessly in the desiccated heat.

The sound of a car door slamming several streets over had her moving, fitting the key to the lock, where the brass slid in so smoothly, almost loosely, that Ellie figured it wouldn't have taken much to pick it, had she been so inclined.

And ten, fifteen years ago, she would have been. Which was why she wasn't particularly eager to be standing around on the street when the next person moseyed on by.

The door opened with a creak, and Ellie winced, her organized brain automatically making a note to grease it up, even though she didn't really care one way or the other. At least, she hadn't thought she did, but as the heavy door croaked its way shut behind her, and she found herself inside a building she hadn't entered for over a decade, she was struck with an undeniable sense of melancholy.

At first glance, the interior of Estelle's Blooms looked exactly the same. But when Ellie tilted her head, looked through the dancing dust motes, she saw that she'd been viewing the small flower shop through the distorted lens of memory.

The forest green shelves full of cheap glass vases, the laminate covered counters. The stack of stained plastic buckets behind the counter, the walk in cooler that someone—thank God—had thought to empty of the bright roses, the painted daisies, the mums and the bundles of baby's breath and leatherleaf and eucalyptus that typically lined the benches inside.

She hadn't been overly excited about the prospect of dealing with the rotten sludge of decaying flowers if no one had thought to clear things out after Estelle's death.

But the cooler was clean, the faintest hint of bleach lingering in the frigid air. And through it, almost hidden in the corner—the door that led to the apartment upstairs. The place Ellie had called home for most of her life.

The place she'd been unceremoniously removed from.

Half turning to go back to her rental car, to get the small bag that held the clothes and toiletries that she'd brought, Ellie instead found herself drawn up the small, rickety staircase, and into the living room of the cramped apartment she'd once shared with Estelle. As with downstairs, things here seemed much the same—the dingy beige carpet, worn down from years of footprints… the peach paint on the walls, a color that had been popular before Ellie had even been born… the ceramic dishes of potpourri so old it had lost its scent. But over it all lay a sense of decay, of neglect, one that

193

combined with the very faint scent of Estelle's perfume to pull at Ellie's skin, drowning her in its intensity.

It was suffocating. Quickly Ellie crossed to the screened window that sat above a television... one so old she'd likely have to hire a crew of neighborhood kids to haul it out for her.

If their parents, once Ellie's contemporaries, would let them have anything to do with her.

She flipped the lock, then put some muscle into turning the handle that cranked the window open. She considered popping the screen out to let more air in, but even if the metal frame hadn't been sealed in place with thick layers of gummy white paint, she doubted it would have done much good.

Years spent in the brisk chill of the Rocky Mountains had wiped the memory of the arid heat away. It was very nearly intolerable, sucking the moisture right from her skin, making her tongue swell with the need for a drink of water.

Good thing she would only been here for a few days. Just long enough to figure out what to do with the mess that Estelle had left behind. She could already feel the anxiety that just being back in this town brought her, pressing down with a weight like water.

The very thought had nausea roiling in her belly. Desperate for a breath of fresh, crisp air that she knew wouldn't come, Ellie nevertheless pressed her face to the dusty mesh screen.

The small street stretched out before her, a black ribbon of tar that she knew would be gooey from baking all day in the sun. In the distance she could see one of the town's nine

194

prisons… if she remembered correctly, it was the one that held Arizona's death row. From this view, the complex consisted of a dismal series of concrete buildings, set far back from a fence made menacing by coils of wire that anyone with a brain knew were far more deadly than they looked.

For the inmates housed in those dull, soul sucking buildings awaiting their punishments, there was no way out. No way past the towers of armed guards, the electrical fence. Though she couldn't condone the things they'd done to be condemned there, Ellie nevertheless felt a sense of kinship with those souls, right in that moment. That hopelessness, the sensation that no matter how fast she ran, she would never make it free of the shackles of her past.

Movement from below caught her eye. Looking down, she watched as a shiny white sedan emblazoned with the word Sheriff ambled down the street. Her pulse picked up just knowing there was a cop in the vicinity, thanks to the rebellious teenage years she'd spent in this very town.

It accelerated even further when the police car pulled up right behind her rental car, a deliberate action on a street that was nearly empty. Ellie listened to her own breath rasping in, shuddering out as time seemed to slow. She watched as a lean, lanky figure in well-worn jeans and a short sleeved blue button down that seemed to have lost some of its crispness in the heat unfolded those long legs from the car and circled her sedate rental, shading his eyes and peering in the driver's side window.

She noted the gun strapped to his hip. When he tucked his hands into his pockets, rocked back on his heels as if chewing something over, he looked right up at the window where she was standing, and her fingers clutched in the dusty curtains, a shock as intense as a lightning bolt nearly brought her to her knees.

Even across the distance that separated them, Ellie could make out the intense green of his eyes—the ultimate confirmation that she was looking at the man who had savagely ripped her heart to shreds.

Not a surprise, really, that he'd followed his father into law enforcement.

He tilted his head to one side, considering, before striding forward, the motion all raw masculinity, pushing through the door to the flower shop beneath. Ellie cursed as her kneejerk reaction whipped through her—she wished she'd locked it, the better to keep him out. And yet...

Wouldn't this be for the best? This man was the reason she had most dreaded coming back to Florence. So she'd get the worst out of the way—no sense in looking over her shoulder the entire time she was here.

The rationale didn't stop her heart from pounding out a wicked tattoo that made her blood pound audibly in her ears.

She couldn't bring herself to turn away from the window, not even when she heard the heavy footfall on the stairs. The tread was familiar, even after nearly ten years.

Some memories, she supposed, left such an imprint on the soul that, while they might recede in intensity from time to time, still never really faded.

As the door at the top of the stairs creaked open, Ellie forced herself to remain still, posed at the window as if she could care less that she was about to see him for the first time since he'd abandoned her. But she couldn't quite calm the trembling of her limbs as adrenaline, pure and potent, shot through her veins, made her feel ill.

"Thought that was you." The voice was straight from her memory, and yet still different—just like the shop, showing how things changed and yet stayed the same. A bit lower, huskier than it had been when they were teenagers. Still sexy enough to smash right on through her carefully constructed walls.

Ellie forced herself to take a long, calming breath before painting the slightest of sneers on her face as she turned. She was a grown woman now, not a child abandoned by her first love just when she'd needed him the most.

She was strong. She'd show him how far she'd come, even if it killed her.

"Gabe." There was no point in being formal, not when she'd once held this man in her arms, had once welcomed him inside of her body. But despite all that, she was proud that she managed to frost his name with just the right amount of disdain. "I don't recall inviting you in."

Damn it. *Damn* it. Since she'd gotten the news of her grandmother's passing, she'd tortured herself with a dozen ways that this first meeting could go, and in all of them she showed him that she'd moved past hurt, and even past hatred, moving right on into indifference—indifference, and not hate, being the ultimate emancipation, after all.

But with those six little words, she'd shown him—shown herself—that she wasn't quite there yet. Pressing her lips together to prevent anything else from slipping out, she crossed her arms over her chest and tried her best to appear as if she couldn't care less whether he stayed or went.

"No, you didn't." Dominic Gabriel—Gabe to those who knew him well—might now be clean shaven, with a tidy haircut and a police car, but the smirk he cast her way was the same, a flash back to the boy who'd been all too eager to be corrupted by the town's only bad girl. He tapped the badge pinned to the front of his shirt, the movement making his biceps flex. "But this did."

"Even a cop can't enter a private property without just cause." Infusing the word *cop* with just a hint of disdain, Ellie arched her eyebrow and tried to tear her stare away from that rock solid arm. When he caught the direction of her gaze he tilted the corners of his lips up again in an arrogant half smile.

"When Mrs. Gunderson calls from next door to tell me that someone is sneaking around Estelle's Blooms and that she and her five cats are terrified, that gives me just cause." Those eyes of his, so bright even in the dimming light, looked her up, then down before settling on her face with an expression that turned it to stone.

And damn it, she could feel her nerves sparking to life everywhere his eyes touched.

"Mrs. Gunderson still lives next door?" Ellie shuddered a bit, remembering the old woman who had been one of the least tolerant of her rebelliousness as a teenager... and that was saying something, since no one in Florence had been particularly tolerant at all. "I would think she'd have recognized me. Since I've always posed such a threat to Muffy and Puffy and Buffy."

Gabe smiled coldly. "Well, you've cleaned right up... on the surface, anyway. No more black hair. No spiked leather, no gothic eyeliner."

You used to love my hair, leather and eyeliner. This was what El-lie wanted to say, but the hardness on Gabe's face stopped her cold. He seemed… angry? With her?

What on earth did *he* have to be angry about? *He* hadn't been forced from his home, his town… he hadn't had to struggle through a searing one two punch of loss as a lonely fifteen year old child.

Her resentment of him ratcheted up a notch, and allowed her to grab hold of her cool defiance with both hands. With a raised chin she nodded towards the door.

"Yes, I've cleaned up my act. But I'm still Estelle's grand-daughter, and I'm here because she just died. She left me the property, so I'm well within my rights to be here. That should ease Mrs. Gunderson's concern. So you can go." Grinding her teeth together, Ellie did her best to keep her voice level, her feelings in check. There was no reason, absolutely none that she should be so upset by seeing Gabe, by having him invade her space. He was a mistake from her past, and she wasn't that girl anymore.

But when he dared to cock his head and let empathy wash over his features, she felt the revolt inside of her turning her stomach in slow circles. How dare he think he knew what she felt? He'd given up that right long ago, when he'd told her without words that he just didn't care.

"Didn't see you at the funeral." Gabe's voice was even, no obvious judgment to be heard. But Ellie knew it was there nonetheless, beating at her with invisible fists.

Once, he'd protected her from that silent judgment. She'd have been silly to expect the same treatment now, but still it shook her.

"And that must have been glaringly apparent, with the whole one or two other people who likely showed up." She regretted the words as soon as they'd left her mouth. She and Estelle had never gotten along, but the old woman had still taken her in, raised her when both her father Joseph and mother Hannah had taken off.

"Ellie. I'm not condemning you. I'm asking why you weren't here then, but are here now." Damn him for looking concerned. It was none of his business. Her *life*, the one she'd forged for herself in the wake of his betrayal, was none of his business.

And still, she found herself spilling her secrets, just as she'd always done. Just one of the things that had sent her, the rebel without a cause, tumbling head first for the town's golden boy so many years before.

Though this time her confession was colored with angry defiance.

"I always let Estelle know when I moved. But she didn't note the last one down, I guess. In her paperwork or her will or whatever. The lawyer had a hard time tracking me down. I didn't get here in time." Though who had thrown her prickly old grandmother a funeral in her stead, Ellie couldn't imagine. The town, she supposed.

It wasn't her fault—she'd been a dutiful granddaughter, if not exactly a warm one, not ever letting the older woman worry about her whereabouts. Not that Estelle would have. And yet Gabe's words had a worm of guilt eating its way through the lining of her gut.

"Hey. Are you okay?" The impenetrable set of his features softened as he seemed to recognize the signs of her inner turmoil. That big, hard body shifted, those feet in their black boots bringing him several steps closer to where she still stood, by the window.

The movement made panic flare to life. She could pretend that she didn't care so long as there was space and angry words between them. But if he touched her... if he came close enough that she could make out that smell that was so uniquely him, the one that had always made her feel safe and cherished and yet excited her immeasurably...

She'd be done for. What that would entail, exactly, she wasn't sure, but she knew it wouldn't be good.

"Well, as you can see, everything here is fine. And as you can also see, I'm no longer the delinquent that I once was, so you don't have to worry about hauling me in for shoplifting or destruction of property." Her voice was unfamiliar even to her, harsh, filled with years of anger and hurt. Where had it come from? She'd felt both of those things when she'd been forced to leave town, certainly. But she'd moved on. Had carved out a decent—no, a *good* life for herself.

Then why did she feel like simultaneously crying and throwing something as she stood here in a room that held so many memories, facing the man who, in her childish innocence, had once been her everything?

"You can go." She added when he simply straightened, looked at her with those damn eyes that had always seen too much. It was as if he knew, even after all this time—as if he could hear the unspoken words in her soul.

And how dare he seem so nonchalant, so unaffected by coming face to face with her when she, despite her best efforts, was torn to shreds inside? It was as if he'd come upon anyone, anyone at all that he'd once known.

It made her want to lash out, to kick and punch and scream just to get some kind of reaction out of him. But with the iron will that she'd been forced to forge after being unceremoniously dumped from her home, Ellie strove to match his impassiveness, nodding when he took a step back.

"I'm sure I'll see you around then." With an answering nod, he strode back across the room, the ugly carpet muffling his footsteps. Ellie bathed in the warm wave of relief at his retreating back, ignoring the baffling disappointment that infused it.

Gabe looked back over his shoulder as his feet hit the top step, and the sexy grin she remembered, tempered with restraint, made her knees shake.

"I hope some of that troublemaking delinquent is still in there, somewhere. Be a damn shame for all that fire to be snuffed out."

And with that he was gone, leaving Ellie staring with a witty—she was sure it was witty—retort on the tip of her tongue. Damn it, she hated being the person who thought up the perfect comeback two hours after the fact.

But perfect or not, witty or not… he was gone.

ACKNOWLEDGMENTS

A book is never just the work of the author. Big thank you's to the following people for their contributions and support!

Jia Gayles... for everything.
Deidre Knight... ditto.
The TKA family.
Jason and Amanda Chalkey, for answering all of my strange prison questions.
Denise Taylor, editor extraordinaire.
Steena Holmes, for soothing my worries.
Suzanne Rock, cause... duh.
Brittany St. Thomas, for answering my scenery questions.
Cindy Turner and Gale Sroelov, for beta reading.
Frauke Spanuth/ Croco Designs for the awesome cover.
Tara Gonzalez/ InkSlinger PR for getting the word out.
Angieleigh Eads for saving my sanity.
Jesse Feldman for helping the plot.
And, of course, my hubby.

About the Author

LAUREN HAWKEYE/LAUREN JAMESON never imagined that she'd wind up telling stories for a living... though when she looks back, it's easy to see that she's the only one who is surprised. Always "the kid who read all the time", Lauren made up stories about her favorite characters once she'd finished a book... and once spent an entire year narrating her own life internally. No, really. But where she was just plain odd before publication, now she can at least claim to have an artistic temperament.

Lauren lives in the Rocky Mountains of Alberta, Canada with her husband, toddler, pit bull and idiot cat, though they do not live in an igloo, nor do they drive a dogsled. In her nonexistent spare time Lauren can be found knitting (her husband claims that her snobby yarn collection is exorbitant), reading anything she can get her hands on, or sweating her way through spin class. She loves to hear from her readers!

Visit Lauren:
www.laurenhawkeye.com
www.laurenjameson.com
twitter: @LaurenHJameson
Facebook: www.facebook.com/LaurenHawkeye

Sign up for Lauren's newsletter to receive new release alerts!

Interested in exclusive excerpts, cover reveals, prizes, man candy and more?
Come join Lauren's Lovelies, my Facebook reader group!